High Stakes Showdown

The young cattleman, Matt Farrell, enjoys his job at the Ferguson Ranch. But the placid routine of ranch work is abruptly shattered one afternoon when he discovers a dead body on the range and simultaneously finds himself at odds with the foreman, McCoy, over the favours of old Ferguson's feisty daughter, Hetty. The conflict heightens when Farrell deliberately humiliates McCoy in a poker game and then gets embroiled against his will in the sheriff's scheme to sort out the mystery of the murdered man.

Now a breathless sequence of events finds Farrell braving a lynch mob, defending himself in a brutal bare-knuckled fight and facing death in a final shoot-out in a spooky Arizona ghost town.

Has he a hope in hell of bucking the odds against him?

By the same author

Settling the Score
Tracks into Terror

High Stakes Showdown

MIKE REDMOND

A Black Horse Western

ROBERT HALE · LONDON

© Mike Redmond 2004
First published in Great Britain 2004

ISBN 0 7090 7480 8

Robert Hale Limited
Clerkenwell House
Clerkenwell Green
London EC1R 0HT

Typeset by
Derek Doyle & Associates, Liverpool.
Printed and bound in Great Britain by
Antony Rowe Limited, Wiltshire

ONE

'Looks like you got a runaway, mister.'

Matt Farrell turned his head abruptly to squint in the direction indicated by McCoy's outstretched arm. A small carousel of dust marked the spot where a maverick had detached itself from the far side of the carefully marshalled herd of young prime beef and was skittering off on a plan of its own through the sagebrush. Farrell cursed, tilted back his hat and drew his shirtsleeve across his brow to clear the sweat – a gesture he had routinely performed a dozen times an hour since early morning. It was late afternoon but the Arizona sun was still beating down remorselessly. They had spent the day cutting out and rounding up young steers for branding. He was hot, tired and impatient for the day to end. The corrals of the Ferguson ranch were less than a mile away and all they had to do was keep the animals moving in a straight line. But there was always one ornery individual who had other ideas.

McCoy was Ferguson's foreman, so an order was an order. But Farrell made a token attempt at protest.

'Why my runaway? It's on Jim's side of the trail, ain't it?'

'Sure,' grunted McCoy. His weather-beaten face was impassive. 'You see him anywhere?'

Today had been a three-man enterprise with Jim Lester,

5

Ferguson's oldest (and, in Farrell's unvoiced opinion, totally pensionable) hand making up the threesome, but as usual he wasn't where he should have been. Farrell shielded his eyes against the sun and just made out Lester's hunched figure way ahead of the lumbering pack, oblivious to anything that was happening behind him and clearly concentrating on being first to the chow table as usual. Farrell choked back the curse he would have liked to pronounce on Lester's inefficiency which habitually made extra work for everyone else – particularly himself as the junior member of the outfit. But McCoy and Lester were pardies and he knew from previous experience that criticism of the old-timer's professional performance would not have been kindly received.

'Guess it's down to me, then.'

But McCoy, confident that his instruction would be obeyed, had already wheeled his horse towards the rear of the herd without waiting for or hearing Farrell's acknowledgement. Farrell set his hat firmly down on his forehead, dug his heels into his horse's flank and set about weaving his way through the ambling steers. It took him a couple of minutes to work his way through, during which he had perforce to take his eyes off the quarry. When he reached the far side the maverick steer was no longer in sight, with nothing but a faint haze of dust to suggest the route it might have taken.

Beyond the fringe of sagebrush and thorn bushes the range gave way to a stretch of falling ground broken by rocky outcrops that eventually led down to a small creek dotted on both sides by cottonwood trees and tangled undergrowth. Farrell picked his way downhill across the scree without even bothering to look for the miscreant's trail. It had obviously smelt water and was intent on treating itself to a drink. When he reached the first of the cottonwoods Farrell checked his horse and paused to look

6

and listen. The sounds of the main body of cattle had faded behind him and for the moment all he could hear was a faint trickle of water up ahead through the bushes and the angry squawking of a few crows disturbed by his approach.

Farrell sat motionless in his saddle for a moment or two, then, at the sound of a muffled snort coming from somewhere to his right he hefted his lariat, checked the suppleness of the noose, and edged his horse forward. The bushy terrain was scarcely ideal for deft ropework but hopefully the animal would be so busy on slaking its thirst that it would let him approach close enough to make a cast at point-blank range. He reached the creek and let his horse pick its way along the edge.

A moment or so later he spotted the white muzzle of the runaway. It was lowered into the water enjoying, as he had anticipated, an unscheduled drink. Farrell checked his horse again while he sized up the situation. The animal was on the opposite side of the creek to him, so a forward approach would have been directly in its line of vision. Farrell wheeled around, retraced his tracks a few yards to place himself outside the steer's sight, and then pushed across the water and some way beyond. Now he had the best chance of approaching his target obliquely from behind. He weaved through some thorn bushes and now the steer was almost directly ahead of him. It raised its head suspiciously as a twig broke under the horse's hoof, stared around, and then resumed its drink.

Farrell leant forward in the saddle, flexing the rope in his right hand. The animal was now within easy range and Farrell held his breath, waiting for the right moment to throw. After a long minute the steer grunted and raised its muzzle from the water. Licking its lips it turned its head and focused its gaze on Farrell. But before it could react, the rope had snaked out and settled round its neck. The animal bellowed as Farrell drew the noose tight and prepared to secure the other end of the rope around his pommel.

Normally the instinctive reaction of a lassoed steer was to pull away from the direction of the snaring rope, but longhorns – particularly juveniles – were never entirely predictable. Farrell, who had been riding the range since he was fifteen, knew all about them. So with nearly ten years experience behind him he should not really have been taken by surprise as the captured animal emitted an indignant snort and charged straight towards him. Alarmed by the sudden skirmish Farrell's horse shimmied to one side and reared slightly, missing its footing on the mud-smeared stones that marked the edge of the creek.

Farrell just had time to mutter a startled oath as the unexpected movement unbalanced him. Tipped from the saddle he sprawled face down on the gravel as his horse skipped out of the path of the enraged steer which now clattered towards him. Despite being winded by the unexpected fall he had sufficient presence of mind to roll out of the way, leaving the beast to charge forward beyond him, obviously intent on escape. But before Farrell could stumble to his feet a socket-wrenching jerk on his right arm reminded him that even in the confusion of his fall he had unconsciously held on to the end of the lasso. So now the roles of captor and captive were momentarily reversed – with the accumulated momentum of the young steer dragging him across the pebbles while Farrell stubbornly grasped the end of the lariat with both hands, mulishly unwilling to let go.

The runaway might have succeeded in pulling itself loose if its path had not been suddenly obstructed by a serried array of thorn bushes. As its onward rush was abruptly checked and the rope went slack Farrell seized the opportunity to get to his feet and brace himself against a cottonwood tree. Before the steer could contrive any further mischief Farrell belayed the end of the rope around the stump of a branch and brought the situation and the escapee under control.

'I oughta bust your hide, mister,' muttered Farrell, brushing dust and mud off his pants under the baleful glare of his captive. He glanced around and was relieved to find that at least his horse had co-operated by declining to hightail it back to the ranch and supper without the company of its master. Instead, it was standing by the side of the creek treating itself to a long drink. Farrell walked over to the animal, preparing to mount up, then clapped his hand to his head with an exasperated click of the tongue: somewhere in the skirmish he had lost his hat. He walked back along the gravelly path he had just traversed involuntarily on his belly, but the hat was nowhere to be seen.

'Rolled in the creek, of course,' said Farrell to nobody in particular. It had been that sort of an afternoon. But his luck was half in, at any rate. The hat was at the water's edge brim down – damp possibly, but not a total casualty. Farrell bent down to retrieve it and then almost leapt back as if he had inadvertently touched a rattlesnake. As he lifted the hat he saw that it was covering a man's hand. Farrell peered down to verify what he was seeing. Squeamishly unwilling to probe with his own bare hands, he used his boot to scuff away the bush that was dipping over the water's edge. The body of a man was lying face down, well concealed under the shrubbery, and it was only by the merest chance that he had come across it. For a moment he stood holding his hat, paralysed with surprise.

'Hey mister.'

Farrell's remark was as inconsequential as the perfunctory prod he administered with the toe of his boot. With his head face down in the muddy trickle the guy was clearly dead and Farrell knew it before he spoke. And if there had been any doubt in his mind the haft of a knife protruding from between the corpse's shoulder blades rendered the matter conclusive.

Wes Ferguson flicked open the case of his gold pocket-watch, checked the time against the clock on the dining-room chimneypiece and uttered an irritated snort. Then he stumped across to his carver chair at the head of the table and drew it back with an angry sweep, grating its feet across the tiles. As he slumped in the chair a trim figure in a starched gingham frock came in through the door that led to the kitchen, bearing a large earthenware casserole.

'Two minutes after six,' muttered Ferguson, running his hand through his thinning grey hair. 'Figured you was planning to starve me to death, missy.'

'Only got one pair of hands, Pa. Had to take Ma's tray up to her and see she took her physic as well. And there's no call to go working up a head of steam – we're not running a railroad timetable.'

Ferguson watched his daughter set the dish on the table.

'Your mother always managed it – supper on the table at six sharp and I could have set the clocks by her. Routine's the only way to manage a ranch. Thought you knew that.' Hetty Ferguson opened her mouth to reply, thought better of it, and sat down to her father's left. She ladled stew into two plates, passed one to her father and they began to eat in silence. After a few mouthfuls Ferguson dabbed a napkin to his mouth, leant back in his chair and gazed at his daughter. The creases of irritation in his face had relaxed.

'Good stew.'

Hetty arched an eyebrow towards him.

'Just like mother used to make it?'

10

'Yeah,' chuckled Ferguson. 'Always knew I had a bright daughter – the kind who learns fast.'

Hetty wriggled with slight embarrassment in her chair, but the upturned corners of her mouth indicated that her father's compliment was not entirely unwelcome.

'Shucks. This is where you'll be telling me I inherited your brains.'

'Sure you did. But you got your mother to thank for your looks. Auburn hair, green eyes, pretty figure. Enough to sweep a man fair off his feet first sight.'

'Some chance. Men are kind of few and far between around the kitchen.'

Ferguson stared at his daughter for a moment and then resumed eating. Only when he had cleared his plate did he pick the topic of the conversation up again.

'Time enough for men. You're only nineteen. Anyways you got one admirer for sure, if I'm not very much mistaken.'

This time it was Hetty's turn to stare.

'What you talking about, Pa? I haven't got no follower. Seems like only yesterday I was still in pigtails.'

'Frank McCoy.'

'Frank? But he's never—'

'Hung about the kitchen, offered to help you at the pump, fetched firewood when he could have got one of the hands to do it. . . . Oh, sure. Of course he hasn't.'

'Oh, that. I never really reckoned. You've got sharp eyes.'

'Of course. And then there's the way he looks at you. Haven't you noticed his eyes following you.'

Hetty cocked her head to one side.

'Can't say I have. Much too busy these days with Ma laid up in bed all consumptive. And anyway Frank's old enough to be my father if I didn't have one already. And no great shakes when it comes to looks.'

11

'As usual, young lady, you exaggerate. Frank's only just turned thirty – even if he do look a tad older. That's what riding the range all day does for you. And he's a hard worker who knows his job. You could do worse.'

'And I could do better. Are you setting up in the match-making business, Pa?'

'Just taking my responsibilities seriously, young lady,' grunted Ferguson, drawing himself up a little in his chair. 'Seems to me you're quite a catch for the right man. Your ma and me ain't going to live for ever and the ranch is all yours when we go. Reckon half the young men in the county ought to be lining up to take your eye and twenty thousand acres of prime range. But you're right about Frank. We ought to be setting your sights higher than a farm foreman. Maybe I should give a dance for you in town like one of them fancy Eastern cotillions. Invite a few beaux, test the market . . .'

'Market? You making me out to be piece of prime beef?'

Ferguson's craggy face relaxed for a moment into an amused grin.

'Don't take it personal. But you do have a value apart from that very pretty face of yours . . .'

He leant back in his chair, reflected for a moment, and then continued his rumination: '. . . But lord only knows where in Pinedale Fork a man could hold a respectable coming-out ball for his daughter. Scarcely think the Goldrush saloon would be kind of fitting.'

Hetty stood up abruptly, her face colouring with embarrassment.

'I . . . I'll see about the coffee.'

She turned towards the kitchen before her father could catch sight of her blushing cheeks. But Ferguson, who had missed nothing, gazed at her retreating back and chuckled quietly into his napkin. In the temporary sanctuary of the kitchen Hetty set about arranging crockery on a tray and then reached for the coffee pot which was already simmering on the stove. In her preoccupation with her father's recent thoughts on matrimony she omitted to use the felt cloth which her mother kept available for handling hot utensils. As she withdrew her hand from the pot with a yelp of pain there was a tap at the kitchen door and Frank McCoy appeared in the threshold.

'Why, Miss Hetty, are you all right?' said McCoy snatching off his hat and eyeing the reddened palm of Hetty's hand.

'What? Oh sure. Just a little singe from the pot handle. My own fault for being careless.'

McCoy stepped forward.

'Will you let me have a look? Can't be too careful with burns.'

'Really, I'm fine. Ain't no call to go making a fuss, Frank.'

Ignoring her dismissive tone McCoy set his hat down on the table and, unbidden, took up her hand, tilting it towards the beams of light from the setting sun streaming in through the window.

'You gotta bit of a burn there, Miss Hetty. Maybe a dab of butter . . . or run it under the cold faucet . . .'

As McCoy's proprietorial finger lingered on her palm for a fraction longer than strictly necessary for visual diagnosis Hetty withdrew her hand from his grasp with an impatient click of the tongue.

'I told you, it's nothing to worry about.'

Before McCoy could make any other move she grasped the potholder and successfully completed her task of loading the coffee tray.

'Something we can do for you, Frank?' she enquired with carefully averted gaze.

13

'Just came to report to Mr Ferguson. Bit late getting back.'

'Oh, of course. He's in the dining-room.'

McCoy nodded and gestured towards the tray. 'Can I help?'

'Just go straight ahead, Frank. I can manage.'

As McCoy shrugged and turned towards the dining-room, Hetty bit her lip as if wondering whether she had been abrupt to the point of actual discourtesy. Then she picked up the tray and followed him out. Wes Ferguson looked up from his reverie at McCoy's respectful tap on the doorframe but remained silent.

'Came to report, Mr Ferguson. We completed the round-up.'

'All right. Any problems?'

'No. Except Farrell.'

'What, fallen off his horse?'

'No, sir. Left him to pick up a stray maverick. Should be tagging along soon.'

Ferguson glanced at the fading daylight through the dining-room window.

'You'd better be right. Don't like a man out alone on the range after dark.'

McCoy squeezed himself against the doorframe to allow Hetty to pass through with the coffee. She set the tray on the table in front of her father, sat down and filled two cups. McCoy hesitated at the door. Some evenings when he made his report Ferguson would invite him to sit down and chew the fat over a cup of coffee and a smoke. But this evening there would evidently be no hospitality. Ferguson stirred his coffee and then looked up as if surprised to see McCoy still standing there.

'Anything else?'

'No, Mr Ferguson.'

'Let me know when Farrell gets back.'

14

'Yes, sir.'

When McCoy was safely out of sight father and daughter exchanged conspiratorial glances.

'Why, Hetty,' remarked the old man, 'Shame on you. You didn't offer Mr McCoy a cup of coffee.'

'There's no shortage of coffee in the cookhouse, Pa. And you wouldn't want me to encourage an unsuitable beau, now would you?'

They continued their desultory banter as the last rays of daylight faded and it was time to turn up the oil-lamps in the parlour. Ferguson was just easing his arthritic frame into his favourite armchair by the log fire when the sounds of a commotion became audible from the direction of the yard. Ferguson cocked his head.

'Reckon that must be Farrell.'

There was silence for a moment outside and then the sound of raised voices followed by a heavy knock at the kitchen door.

'That'll be your beau comin' to report, Hetty. Don't keep him waiting, now.'

Hetty bustled out, to reappear a few moments later with McCoy behind her. Ferguson looked up.

'Farrell OK?'

'Yes, sir. But—'

'But what? Lost the maverick, I suppose. Tell him we'll dock his—'

'No sir. The steer's fine. It's just that he's brought back . . . Well, I guess you should come and look.'

Ferguson stared at his foreman in perplexity, took immediate note of the seriousness of his expression, and followed him outside without a further word. McCoy led him to the barn, where Farrell was standing by a trestle-table holding an oil-lamp in one hand.

'What in tarnation?' muttered Ferguson, stumping across to where Farrell was standing.

'I . . . er . . . found this down by the creek, Mr Ferguson, Didn't seem kind of right to leave it lying out there, so I slung it over my horse and brought it in.'

The body was lying face up on the table, its bloodless face illuminated by the oil-lamp.

'Jesus,' said Ferguson, peering down. 'He won't be riding the range no more. Must have fallen and cracked his skull or something.'

Farrell shook his head. 'Sir, I don't think so.'

'Oh, you got a better—'

Ferguson's reply was cut short as Farrell indicated a bloodstained Bowie knife which was lying in the shadows beside the body.

'I found it stuck in his shoulder blades and it sure didn't get there by accident.'

Ferguson's gaze passed from the knife, to Farrell and back to the body again. Then he beckoned McCoy.

'Anyone claiming to recognize him?'

'Nope.'

'We'll have to take him into town in the morning and see what Sheriff Finch makes of it. Meantime cover him up with a tarpaulin.'

As McCoy busied himself with arrangements for covering the body Ferguson walked out of the barn with Farrell just behind him.

'You eaten yet, boy?'

'No sir. I was just goin' to check what was left in the cookhouse.'

'Cold chow and tepid coffee if you're lucky. Here, come back to the house. I reckon my daughter can improve on that.'

They walked across to the ranch-house where Hetty was standing on the stoop peering into the gathering darkness.

'This young fella's just salvaged a corpse on our land.

16

Told him you could fix him up with some hot grub. You ain't about to disappoint him, I hope.'

Hetty's jaw dropped. 'A corpse? Well, sure . . . if Mr Farrell doesn't mind taking pot luck with the remains of the stew. I can easily—'

' 'Course he doesn't mind,' grunted Ferguson. 'Lucky to get it. Now inside, both of you.'

'Take a seat in the dining-room, Mr Farrell,' said Hetty indicating a door to the right, 'I'll be with you in a moment.'

'The dining-room?' queried Farrell in an anxious tone. 'But Miss Hetty I haven't washed up . . . and . . . my boots . . . the kitchen'd be fine with me.'

'Shucks, son,' said Ferguson, prodding him none too gently in the spine. 'I asked you in here for a meal. We don't expect guests to eat in the kitchen. And I'm sure my daughter will be willing to take a chance on your boots. Besides, I want to hear the full story and with my arthritis I sure ain't fixing to hear it standing up.'

'Of course I'll take a chance with the boots,' said Hetty, surveying Farrell from head to foot. Her stare was appraising, but not disapproving. His clothes were dishevelled and he was clearly a few hours away from a decent shave, but his blue eyes looked sharp under a mop of dark hair, and he was holding himself straighter than was usual for anyone who had just spent a long day in the saddle.

Suddenly uncomfortable under Miss Hetty's cool gaze, Farrell shrugged, turned into the dining-room and subsided as bidden into a chair. Any misgivings he might have felt about being in no fit state to sit at a decent dining-table were soon dispelled by the dispensation of a large helping of stew accompanied by some really strong black coffee. Under his hostess's ministrations Farrell's tiredness diminished as his belly filled, but no attempt at conversation was made until Farrell had been served his

17

second mug of coffee. Then Ferguson, who had been sitting in his usual carver chair, leant forward and pushed a rosewood humidor across the table.

'Smoke?'

'Why, thanks very much, sir.'

Farrell opened the box and selected the smallest cigar he could see. When they had both lit up, Ferguson cocked an impatient eyebrow towards him.

'Well, get on with it, son. Let's hear the whole story.'

'Oh, yeah . . . sure.'

Farrell paused and glanced enquiringly at Miss Hetty, who was sitting at the table opposite him. Ferguson snapped his fingers impatiently.

'Don't mind her for Pete's sake. She's a rancher's daughter – seen and heard everything.'

'Well, in that case . . .' Farrell grinned across the table, 'I guess I needn't be selective about the detail.'

When he had finished his account Ferguson leant back in his chair and exhaled a smoke ring towards the ceiling.

'Seems to me we don't know much unless one of the other hands recognizes this cahoot. We can't even be sure when he died.'

'Body was cold when I got to him. And of course half of him had been doused in the creek anyway. But it must have happened in the last twenty-four hours.'

'Oh?' Ferguson's brow had furrowed again. 'What makes you think that?'

'Because as far as I could make out, the body's intact. Hasn't been . . . er . . . you know . . . touched by anything.'

'Right. And how did he get there? Any sign of a horse?'

'No. But what with me and the antics of that maverick the ground was all scuffed up. I didn't get a proper look.'

'Could have been a stray Apache, I suppose. Decent horse and saddle would be worth a fair bit down south if he didn't want it for himself.'

Farrell shook his head.

'You're forgetting something. Apaches would never have left the knife in his back.'

Ferguson nodded. 'All right. So I got an unknown visitor stabbed to death on my property. About how old, would you say?'

'Late twenties maybe. Difficult to say.'

'Did you go through his pockets?'

'Yep. A few greenbacks and coins. But nothin' to show who he was.'

Ferguson sighed. 'This is one for the sheriff. We'll sling Mr Unknown on the buckboard tomorrow morning and take him into town. At least he can get a decent burial. You can tell the mortician to charge a plain pine coffin to my account.'

Farrell stared across at him.

'Me?'

'Why yes. You found him so you've got the most to tell. I'm sure Jade Finch'll be mighty interested to hear all about it – specially as he always reckons the fella who found the body usually committed the crime. You got any problem with a day in town tomorrow – better than stamping cattle, surely?'

'Guess not,' conceded Farrell.

'Good,' said Ferguson, levering himself out of his chair. 'In that case I'll bid you goodnight. See the cowboy out, Hetty.'

Farrell followed Hetty out through the kitchen where she unbolted the door and held it open for him. As he was about to pass through she put a hand lightly on his arm.

'Don't mind what Pa said about you finding the body. He likes his little jokes.'

'What? Oh, no I didn't think anything of it.'

Farrell smiled and hesitated at the door, searching for some pretext to prolong the moment. 'Though I was a bit

19

surprised to hear he had an account at the mortician's.
Kind of suggests you got a high death rate around here.'

This time it was Hetty's turn to smile.

'It's not that macabre. Joe Doyle's only the mortician
part-time. He's also the carpenter and timber merchant.
Pa does a lot of business with him.'

'Phew. That sure eases my mind.'

Farrell stepped out into the yard.

'Guess I'll say good night then. And thank you for the
hospitality.'

'You're welcome. Good night, Mr Farrell.'

'It's Matt, if you like.'

'Oh. Good night, then, Matt.'

Satisfied with the modest progress he appeared to have
made with his hostess, Farrell clamped on his hat as the
kitchen door closed behind him, and picked his way
through the darkness to the bunkhouse. He had just
turned the corner of the barn wall when a hand grasped
his shoulder from behind.

'What the. . . ?'

Farrell turned in surprise and peered into the gloom.

'Oh, it's you,' he said, making out the figure of Frank
McCoy. 'You kinda gave me a scare. Something wrong?'

'Maybe, maybe not.' McCoy's voice was thick with
scarcely suppressed tension. His grip tightened on
Farrell's shoulder as he thrust him none too gently against
the barn wall. 'Seems like you enjoyed your fancy dinner
with Miss Hetty. I saw you back there by the kitchen looking pretty cosy with her.'

'Hey,' protested Farrell, trying to shake off McCoy's
hand. 'The boss gave me a meal, that's all. You got any
objection?'

'No. Unless it includes canoodling with his daughter
back of the house.'

'Mighty nice of you to act as chaperon for me, Frank –

but you've figured it wrong,' said Farrell, dimly perceiving what McCoy was getting agitated about. McCoy's vice-like grip was annoying and he tried to wrench himself away. As McCoy persisted in his hold, Farrell's temper boiled over.

'In any case, if Miss Hetty cares to talk to me I don't see what it's got to do with you. I didn't notice your hat hanging in the hall.'

'Yeah? Then you need to get wise, mister,' muttered McCoy through clenched teeth, 'and a sight less sassy. Maybe this'll encourage you.'

He slammed Farrell viciously back against the barn wall and as Farrell's head met the timbers with a hollow thud he stepped back and delivered a haymaking punch into Farrell's undefended stomach. The speed and violence of the onslaught left Farrell unable to do more than fold in two like a sack of coal, with a sharp grunt of pain and surprise. He sagged against the woodwork, as the stew which he had so recently ingested in the cosy intimacy of the Fergusons' dining-room forced its way back through his gullet in a helpless choking eruption of vomit. Before collapsing half-dazed at McCoy's feet he just had time to reflect on the cruel waste of Miss Hetty's cooking.

TWO

Pinedale Fork was a bustling little cattle town of some 3,000 people which owed much of its current prosperity to its position at the fork of the Pine River, and the recent arrival of a railhead less than twenty miles to the north. Saturday mornings usually got off to a quiet start following the inevitable high jinks of a Friday night when the local cowpokes converged to splurge their pay on the customary recreational activities. Today, however, the sound of hammering echoed down main street before most of the local shopkeepers had got their shutters down. Outside the clapboard building adjacent to the Goldrush saloon a team of carpenters was busy dislodging the discrete sections of a faded panel attached to the façade at second-floor level which had previously announced PINEDALE TRAVELLERS TEMPERANCE INN.

'Careful, boys,' warned a portly shirtsleeved figure who was supervising activities from the sidewalk. 'Some good reusable timber in those old panels. Take those nails out real easy, now.'

'OK, Mr Doyle,' acknowledged one of the hands from his temporary perch some fifteen feet above street level. 'They're coming away clean as whistle.'

'Glad to hear they're respecting my property,' remarked a clear strong voice to Doyle's right. He turned

22

and doffed his black hat towards a well-built woman in a crimson taffeta dress who had appeared at the balustrade of the Goldrush saloon and was craning her head upwards to survey the work in hand.

'Morning, Mrs Carney. Boys'll have your new sign up in next to no time.'

He gestured to the back of an open wagon parked alongside on which were laid three panels – of larger dimensions and significantly louder lettering than those which were being removed – which, when assembled in correct sequence, would proclaim PINEDALE GOLDRUSH HOTEL.

'Morning, Joe,' said Beth Carney, turning towards him. 'Stage gets in at eleven – which is when I'm fixing to have the doors open. Kind of important to have the joinery all complete. Business is business.'

'Sure thing,' said Doyle casting a professional eye over the newly renovated façade of the erstwhile temperance lodgings. 'I think we done you a real good job here. And on time, too.'

'Just.' Beth Carney pursed her lips. 'Let's hope it's on budget, too. I'll find out soon enough when you sends in your bill.'

'No worry, ma'am. Won't cost you a penny extra than I quoted.'

Beth nodded, turned and made her way back into the Goldrush. She crossed the main saloon where a couple of Mexican maids were sweeping up the detritus of last night's activities and laying out fresh sawdust and cuspidors, and passed through a door at the rear which led to her office. A large mahogany desk, its surface devoid of either clutter or embellishment, stood at the window which was heavily draped with brocade and lace. At the other side of the room stood a leather-topped table strewn with stacks of coins and piles of greenbacks at which an elderly man in a threadbare blue-serge suit was stooped with a pencil and notebook in hand.

'You about done, Zach? I got a busy morning.'

Beth took her seat behind the desk and tilted her chin imperiously in the direction of the table.

'Yes, ma'am. Five hunnerd and ninety-three dollars and seventy-two cents on the nail. Care to check my reckoning?'

Beth shook her head. 'Just bag it up.'

Zach Granger shot a quick glance across at her as he straightened himself and lodged the pencil behind his ear. The sunlight filtering through the heavily shaded window cast flattering highlights on her immaculately coiffed auburn hair and her handsome largely unlined face bore only the slightest trace of feminine artifice. Only a tell-tale spreading of her figure, held ruthlessly in check by the application of the best whalebone stays supplied to order by a couturier in Chicago, hinted that she might have passed her fortieth birthday. But this was only to be surmised since she never vouchsafed any personal information (and no one would have been imprudent or indelicate enough to make a direct enquiry). Only some of the older-established residents were able to recall that she was scarcely out of her teens when she had arrived off the overland stage as a penniless bargirl some twenty years previously. And nobody could exactly pin down the moment when Beth had made the transition from being a mere *Miss* to a more substantial *Mrs* – a change in status apparently unmarked by the formal processes of matrimony. But it didn't matter: the townsfolk of Pinedale Fork were ready to accept the steady progress of her material circumstances from servant to proprietor as a demonstration of business acumen which fully entitled her to be taken at her own valuation.

And as the town had prospered, so had she. The

Goldrush had gone from strength to strength, and the most recent manifestation of its success had been Beth's acquisition (*rescuing* had been her own ironic description of the purchase) of the adjacent temperance hotel which had been opened with high, and pious, hopes by a family of Quaker entrepreneurs from further east some five years previously. But their sober aspirations had totally failed to match the commercial and social realities of the location and the times.

Zach slid open one of the table's two drawers, and produced a selection of cloth bags into which he deftly stowed the sorted notes and coins. The bags were then stuffed into a heavy canvas satchel with a brass lock. He took this across to Beth's desk, where she extracted a small key from her reticule. She applied this to the lock, stood up and handed the bag back to Granger.

'Let's go. Mustn't keep old Weizman waiting.'

Saturday mornings at the Goldrush followed an invariable ritual. Before the rest of the town was fully astir Zach would tally up the takings and escort Beth across to the Cattlemen's Bank where the money would be paid in. Such was Beth's commercial standing in Pinedale Fork that there was never any question of her suffering the indignity of being kept waiting at the grille while the teller dealt with a prior customer. At precisely nine o'clock the chief cashier would be waiting to receive Beth in the foyer and would then escort her through a pass door to the inner sanctum where the proprietor, Mr Theo Weizman, dressed in impeccable grey worsted frock-coat, would rise gravely from behind his desk, settle Beth in the comfortable leather armchair opposite and exchange polite banalities with her while the cashier and Zach completed the formalities of paying in. With the paperwork reconciled and agreed Mr Weizman would issue, sign and stamp a receipt under his own hand and pass it across to Beth with a word of commendation on the continuing prosperity of her business. He would then make bold to enquire whether the bank could be of any other small service, to which Beth would invariably reply in the negative. (Even the purchase of the Temperance Hotel had been accomplished without the necessity of Beth adding her name to the extensive roll of Weizman's local mortgagees.) Hands would be shaken and Beth would take her leave until the following week.

Zach held open the office door, but before passing through, Beth paused to select a black-lace mantilla from the adjacent hatstand. This she draped decorously over her head with minimum disturbance to her carefully arranged hair. The bank was no more than a few steps across the street, but Beth would never venture even such a short journey without being properly covered in deference both to the canons of public taste and to the formality of Theo Weizman's frock-coat.

At the edge of the boardwalk Zach offered Beth his free arm and selected the straightest possible path across the street to Mr Weizman's premises consistent with the avoidance of any ruts, mud, puddles or equine effluvia which might otherwise have soiled her elegant slippers. Main Street in Pinedale Fork had been kept deliberately wide in order to facilitate the driving of cattle from one end of town to the other, and they had picked their way about half-way across when Beth became vaguely aware of a horseman cantering towards them. Concentrating of necessity on the safe and hygienic placement of her feet she failed to look up as the horse's hoofs accelerated and the rider bore down on them, knocking Zach against her while the rider, in one deft swoop, leant forward from his saddle, punched Zach's head and grabbed the canvas bag from his unresisting hand. As Beth and Zach stumbled to the ground in an inelegant tangle the rider made off at full gallop.

The snatch had been accomplished at lightning speed but even from her recumbent position Beth had sufficient presence of mind to summon immediate assistance.

'Hey, stop him someone – he's got my takings.'

The scattering of early morning bystanders on both sides of the street stood frozen for a moment as they digested the tableau. Then someone shouted: 'Fetch the sheriff.' A young boy detached himself from the group and ran off towards the sheriff's office, while a couple of gentlemen who had emerged from the barber's shop hastened across to offer assistance.

'You all right, ma'am?' enquired one man, stooping to offer Beth his hand.

'I'm fine,' she said, getting to her feet. 'But that ain't the point. Thievin' varmint just got away with my takings. And look what he done to Zach.'

She pointed down to her escort who was lying face down in the dust. His hat had become detached in the mêlée, revealing a streak of blood on his temple. And for the moment at least he was motionless.

As usual Matt Farrell had been wide awake long before the breakfast horn had sounded at seven o'clock. He had crawled into his bunk the previous night with a sore head and an aching gut, but despite his tiredness sound sleep had eluded him. McCoy had stridden away from the scene of their altercation without another word, leaving Farrell to pick himself up and collect his wits, but it seemed unlikely that the episode would have no sequel. Farrell had lain on his back staring into the darkness while the snores of the other occupants of the bunkhouse reverberated around him.

Until that evening he had been quite unaware that McCoy entertained any feelings for Miss Hetty or that there was anything in the nature of an understanding between them. He also dared to wonder whether Miss Hetty shared McCoy's view of the situation. As his mind engaged with this conundrum he also perforce found himself examining his own feelings about the evening's events. Supper in the comfort of a real dining-room, with decent furniture, clean napery and the soft illumination of shaded oil-lamps, would have been a rare and welcome treat in itself. But when combined with the company of a clean, pretty, well-spoken young lady it was positively inspirational. A man could endure a long hard day in the saddle with perfect equanimity if he knew he was coming back to that sort of domesticity every night. No wonder McCoy was anxious to stake out a claim.

Farrell had tossed and turned uncomfortably as he reflected that that one brief hour in the Fergusons' company represented all the simple delights that had been conspicuously absent from his own life in the last few years. He was suddenly aware that time was slipping past with very little to show for endless days of hard work as someone else's employee. How much more urgent must the situation seem for McCoy, who was at least four or five years his senior.

He also found himself wondering whether he had been right to offer no resistance to McCoy. Of course, the assault had taken him unfairly by surprise, but he could have picked himself up and made a proper fight of it, if that was what McCoy wanted. As the younger man Farrell would have fancied himself every time one to one against McCoy. But then he also knew from personal experience that before committing yourself in bunkhouse disputes you had to consider both the opponent and the situation. McCoy had cronies amongst the hands, and in any case they all depended on him for their jobs. If Farrell chose to make a stand, the most likely outcome would be to find himself pinioned against a wall one night by a couple of willing henchmen while the foreman used him as a punch-bag prior to running him off the ranch. He had watched it happen to others often enough.

Neither of them made any reference to the previous night's spat when they met at breakfast, and if any of the hands were aware of what had happened nobody alluded to it. Anyway, Ferguson had decreed that it should be Farrell who would take the dead body into town, so there was no need for McCoy to give him any instructions for the routine work of the day.

At eight o'clock the buckboard was duly wheeled out and rigged up. After the corpse had been inspected by the other hands in full daylight and failed to elicit any recognition, it was covered by a length of tarpaulin and conveyed with a perfunctory show of reverence to the wagon. Farrell climbed aboard and flicked the reins. Ferguson had effectively given him leave of absence for the day so it would be a welcome chance to escape from the smoky drudgery of cattle-branding and utilize a bit of spare time to marshal his own still-confused thoughts.

It was a journey of some three miles to Pinedale Fork, and Farrell let the horse set its own leisurely pace. So it was just approaching nine o'clock when the wagon rumbled past the first of the scattered houses that marked the entrance to town. The road led slightly downhill for a quarter of a mile or so, and then turned right. At this point the buildings on either side became continuous and the road became Main Street. Farrell had worked at the Ferguson ranch for nearly a year and had become reasonably familiar with the layout of Pinedale Fork – mainly through the usual Friday and Saturday night forays with the other hands in search of diversion and an opportunity to spend their pay. In practice this rarely involved calls at more than two establishments – first the barber for a weekly trim and a shave with a properly honed razor, and then the Goldrush saloon where food, drink and feminine company were available at a range of prices to suit all pockets.

Farrell turned the corner, keeping the buckboard more or less in the centre of the street where it seemed less rutted – not that considerations of a smooth ride were of any account to his defunct passenger. As he proceeded along, scanning the buildings on either side for the sheriff's office he suddenly became aware of a commotion a couple of hundred yards ahead of him. Almost in the blink of an eye he had a confused impression of a fast-moving horse, a couple crossing the street, the horse swerving, the couple in a tangled heap and then a general cry of '*stop him*' as the rider at the centre of the mêlée charged towards him at full gallop.

Scarcely pausing to think, Farrell instinctively slewed the buckboard round so that it partially obstructed the oncoming fugitive's path. The rider checked the horse's pace slightly so as to swerve round the obstruction and as he did so Farrell dropped his reins, stood up, and launched himself blindly at him, with the vague idea of getting his arms around the fellow's midriff. His vault was mistimed, however, and he only succeeded in catching hold of the rider's leg. Dragged violently from the buckboard by the speed of the oncoming horse Farrell hung on desperately as the startled animal was spurred forward. His boots trailing in the dirt, and his arms feeling as if they had almost been wrenched from their sockets, Farrell thought that he was going to have to let go: the momentum of the horse was simply too much for him. But the rider was reining single-handed while clutching what looked like a bag under his other arm, and now Farrell's weight and tenacity succeeded in unbalancing him and dislodging his boot from the stirrup shoe. Dropping the reins, but unwilling to release the bag, he fell to the ground with Farrell grimly holding on to his boot. With a wild oath he kicked at Farrell's jaw with his free leg, forcing Farrell to release his grip. He stumbled to his feet and spun round to face his adversary.

'Ya interfering son-of-a-bitch,' he yelled from behind the neckerchief that was concealing the lower part of his face. 'I'll bust you in pieces.'

As he turned he reached clumsily for the pistol that hung by his right arm, but Farrell was way ahead of him.

'Don't waste your time, mister,' he snarled from his position flat in the dirt. The masked man froze in mid-draw as he became aware that despite the inconvenience of his position Farrell had somehow managed to slick his own revolver out of its holster and was even now levelling it at his chest. The would-be thief stared at Farrell for a moment, glanced around at both sides of the street where a sizeable group of onlookers, some of them armed, had appeared as if by magic, decided that neither resistance nor flight was possible, and flung the canvas bag to the ground with another oath.

'Nice work, mister,' remarked a calm voice from the sidewalk as Farrell got to his feet keeping his revolver trained on the would-be thief. A stocky figure in black vest and pants, wearing a silver star on his chest, detached himself from the shadows and walked across to the frozen tableau in the middle of the street. Farrell recognized him from previous generally friendly encounters in the bar of the Goldrush saloon as Jade Finch, the county sheriff. Finch approached the miscreant and relieved him of his gun. Then he flicked aside the kerchief that was covering the lower half of his face. He stood revealed as a young lad still in his teens with a weak pock-marked face under wispy corn-coloured hair.

'Trash,' remarked the sheriff in even tones, bringing down the boy's own pistol across his face and sending him

31

reeling backwards into the arms of one of his assistants who promptly applied a pair of handcuffs to his wrists.

'You recognize him?' asked Farrell.

'Not specially,' said Finch. 'But we been havin' a bit of trouble from some characters from the wrong end of town lately. Ain't hard to guess where he comes from. Problem is we got a fair amount of railroad building in the vicinity and it brings entirely the wrong sort of people.' The sheriff stared at Farrell. 'Say, don't I know you, son?'

'Matt Farrell, from Ferguson's.'

'Oh, right. Thought your face was familiar, 'cept of course I'm used to seeing it through a cloud of tobaccy smoke down at the Goldrush. You look kind of healthier in broad daylight.'

Finch chuckled at his own joke and then added, 'Real slick piece of work you jumping off that buckboard. And dangerous – you could have fallen clean under the horse.'

'Never gave myself time to think about it,' said Farrell modestly. 'Just went ahead and dived for him.'

'Yeah, well I guess we're beholden to you. Or rather . . . she is.' Finch pointed down the street, where Beth Carney, on her feet again and, with dignity at least partially restored, was striding towards them.

'Hey, Jade,' she called as she approached. 'You string that varmint up good and high. He just caught old Zach a real wallop. Fair knocked the old-timer senseless. We ain't got room in this town for that sort of trash.'

'Wait a minute,' protested the captive, as Beth's words were accompanied by a chorus of approval from the assembled bystanders, 'I ain't killed nobody. Gimme a chance will ya?'

'Sure,' said Finch. 'In front of a judge. Nice and legal.'

Before the crowd could work itself up into a lather he nodded briskly to his assistant. 'Get him inside. I got some questions to ask.'

As the boy was frog-marched away Farrell holstered his Colt, retrieved the satchel from the ground, dusted it off and handed it to Beth.

'Yours I think, ma'am.'

'You bet it is.'

Beth grabbed the bag and peered at Farrell.

'Oh, it's you, Matt. I saw what you did. Mighty quick thinkin', if I may say so. Seems like this town's getting a tad risky for a lady going about her legitimate business.' She shot a withering glance at Finch, who promptly shook his head.

'Told you before to vary your routine, Beth – but you're too pigheaded to listen. Times is a-changing.'

'Yes – and not necessarily for the better.'

'Well,' said Farrell, deciding to intervene before the exchange could heat up, 'If there's anything else I can do for you . . .'

'Sure there is,' said Beth. ' You can help me complete my business which was so rudely interrupted. There's the bank and here's my arm. You can take me over there. It'd be kind of reassuring,' she added, with another backward glance at the sheriff, 'to have a real man to squire me.'

As she offered her arm Farrell smiled and bowed with mock gallantry. 'Ain't no street for a lady to walk down in fine shoes, ma'am. Let me drive you the rest of the way.' He gestured politely to the buckboard.

'Why, thank you, Mr Farrell,' she replied with a wink and the merest suspicion of a curtsy.

He steered her over to the buckboard, but as she prepared to mount to the front bench her eye fell on the contents behind the seat and she clutched at Farrell's hand with a horrified shriek. Farrell glanced down and saw with dismay that the abrupt slewing of the wagon as he had diverted it to head off the fleeing boy had partially dislodged the dead body from its covering, so that the

33

face, its rictus stretched tight, was now grotesquely exposed to the bright sunlight.

'Oh, ma'am,' began Farrell, 'I'm real sorry . . .'

But another cry from Beth cut short his shamefaced apology.

'You got a body in that wagon.'

'Well, yes. I was . . .'

Beth's elegantly manicured fingernails were cutting into Farrell's palm. He winced as he tried to find a few adequate words to explain the situation.

'I'm real sorry if it took you by surprise. Fact is—'

'Surprise?' Beth stared at him. 'That ain't the half of it. Mister, that's my own brother.'

THREE

'Just as I was figurin' on having a quiet Saturday morn-ing . . .'

The tone in Jade Finch's voice was mildly reproachful as he leant back in his chair and surveyed the two figures seated in front of him. Matt Farrell, covered from head to foot in dust from his recent exertions, sat on an upright chair dangling his hat between his knees, while Beth Carney, who had been accorded the privilege of occupying the only padded leather armchair in the premises, sat alongside with the canvas bag in her lap. She had produced a tiny lace handkerchief with which, for the sake of feminine decorum, she dabbed intermittently at her eyes. But as yet it betrayed no sign of dampness. Farrell had recounted the circumstances of his mission to town, and the sheriff now turned his attention to Beth.

'Any idea as to how your brother might have come to be face down in a creek with a knife in his back?'

Beth snorted. 'Kind of thought that was your depart-ment, Jade. I ain't seen him in five years – and that was in Kansas City.'

'No need to get uppity, Beth. I can understand it's been a bit of a surprise.'

'Surprise that young Matt here found him with a knife in his back. Not a surprise that he was in the area, though.'

Finch's eyebrows arched slightly.

'How so?'

'Because he wrote to me a while back saying he was coming out.'

'Give any reason?'

'No.'

'And did you write back?'

'No. He didn't give an address. And anyway, I figured he'd turn up when he turned up. That was usually the way. Didn't expect him to appear flat out in a buckboard though. That was kind of a shock.'

Finch nodded.

'Guess I should offer you my condolences—'

'Condolences, shucks,' interrupted Beth. 'Told you I hadn't seen him in five years – and that was the first time in another five. Fact is we never had much time for each other. And when he did show his face it was usually because he was in some kind of trouble and wanted money.'

She sat back in her chair with a slight sigh, as if relieved to have got this minor family revelation off her chest. 'Wouldn't have wished him to finish like this, of course,' she added as a hurried afterthought, possibly fearing that her previous denial of sisterly affection might have suggested a motive for fratricide.

'Sure,' said Finch. 'You still got the letter?'

'Why in tarnation would I keep something like that? I already told you we weren't normally on corresponding terms. If you're suspecting—'

'No need to get all sassy, Beth. I ain't about to detain you.'

'Well I'm sure glad to hear it—'

'As a matter of fact,' continued Finch without allowing her to finish her sentence, 'I'd be more likely to put my finger on Farrell here as he found the body.'

As Finch's gaze switched to the seated cowboy Farrell sprang to his feet.

'Hey, wait a minute, I didn't . . .'

Finch waved him back into his chair with a dismissive chuckle.

'Take it easy, son. I was just ruminating on the old sheriff's saying that the guy who found the body generally did the deed. Ain't you ever heard that?'

'Yes, I have as a matter of fact,' said Farrell. 'And I didn't find it any funnier the first time.'

There was silence for a moment as Farrell glared at the sheriff and then resumed his seat.

'Anyway,' continued Finch, 'I think we got an explanation as to how . . . Mr . . . er . . .' He broke off in some confusion and turned back to Beth. 'Excuse me, ma'am, I don't think you told us your brother's name.'

'Jake.'

'Jake. And the . . . er . . . family name?' A note of coy delicacy had crept into the sheriff's voice.

Beth shrugged. 'Weren't kind of relevant. He had a name for every occasion. Last time we spoke he was known as Jake Sibley.'

'Right,' said Finch. 'Well, as I was saying, I think we know how your brother got to the creek. Stray horse was picked up all saddled and bridled on the edge of town yesterday. Guy who found it turned it into the stables thinking it might be one of theirs, but it wasn't. I sent a man out along the trail aways to see if anyone had had an accident but he didn't find anything. Obviously he didn't look far enough.'

'That's something, at least,' said Farrell. His glance fell on the Bowie knife and the small amount of money that lay on the sheriff's desk. 'Otherwise there doesn't seem much to go on.'

'Nope,' agreed Finch. 'Of course I'll have a proper look

at the body when Joe Doyle's got him laid out neatly.'

'Oh,' said Farrell, turning towards Beth, 'that reminds me, ma'am. Mr Ferguson said any funeral arrangements was to be put to his account, but that was before . . . I mean . . .'

'You mean that blood's thicker than water and that obligations is obligations.'

Farrell coloured with embarrassment. 'Well, I wasn't going to put it as straight as that.'

Beth laughed. 'Save your blushes, cowboy. I'm a businesswoman – you should know that. Tell Wes Ferguson we won't be troubling his account.'

She tucked her still-dry handkerchief into her sleeve and stood up.

'Well, I guess if Sheriff Finch here isn't fixing to lock either of us up, we might as well get on with what's left of the day.'

She strode out of the office with the satchel under her arm and Farrell close behind her.

'I guess I'll bid you good morning, then, ma'am,' said Farrell as they stepped out on to the boardwalk. 'Unless there's anything else . . .'

Beth turned and looked him up and down.

'You bet there is, mister. You were about to escort me to the bank before I spotted your passenger. We still haven't got there.'

She grasped his arm and turned him in the direction of the bank. Finch had deputed one of his assistants to take the buckboard and its cargo down to the mortician, so they walked the short distance. Inside the bank the chief cashier looked up from his paperwork and bustled across.

'Mrs Carney. Sure sorry about what—'

' 'T'ain't nothing,' said Beth with impatience, tapping the bag of money. 'Where's Zach?'

'Doc Wilson took him off. Reckoned he was a bit

concussed. Will you step right in, ma'am?'

The cashier ushered Beth towards the pass door, interposing himself between her and Farrell. Beth noticed the manoeuvre and immediately stretched out her hand to motion Farrell alongside.

'He comes with me. Escort stays till I've got my receipt – you know the routine.'

'Certainly.'

The cashier gave the dusty and dishevelled Farrell a withering glance, but nevertheless ushered them both across the threshold of Theo Weizman's inner sanctum. Beth cut short Weizman's conventional expression of solicitude by dropping the bag on the table and turning to the cashier.

'Best get counting. I've lost an hour this morning already.'

When the money had been stacked and the total agreed, Weizman prepared to write out the usual receipt.

'Just a moment,' said Beth. 'Hand back fifty dollars.'

The cashier looked surprised, but counted out fifty dollars in greenbacks and handed them over.

'Not to me,' said Beth with a dismissive wave of her hand. 'Give them to Mr Farrell here. Seems to me he's earned them.'

'Now just a moment, ma'am,' protested Farrell, 'I wasn't angling for no reward when I—'

'Sure you weren't. Which is exactly the reason why a token of appreciation is incumbent on me. So you take it. Mr Weizman here will confirm I can afford it. Ain't that so, Theo?'

Weizman smiled gravely and inclined his head.

'Certainly. And I think a word of appreciation to Mr Farrell on behalf of the bank would not be inappropriate either. That was sharp thinking and sharp action out there. Seems to me we're indebted to you, young man.

Town's getting livelier by the month and the sheriff . . .'

Weizman checked himself, as if unwilling to give expression to any sentiment that might reflect adversely on the professional capabilities of the local law enforcement officer.

'. . . Isn't getting any younger.' Beth completed the sentence for him with reasonable tact. She turned Farrell, who was already pocketing the money, towards the door. 'See you next week, Theo. Local trash permitting. . . .'

When they were outside Farrell made to escort Beth across the road to the saloon, but she brushed aside his hand.

'What you doing, mister?'

'Well, I was fixing to see you back and maybe . . .'

'Spend some of that money on liquor at my bar?'

Farrell smiled.

'Something like that.'

'Forget it, cowboy. Have you seen the state of your clothes? Ain't fit for a scarecrow. First thing you do is go off to the outfitters and get yourself a whole new rig, charging to my account. I ain't having you in my saloon with half the dirt of Main Street sticking to your hide.'

She wrinkled her nose suspiciously.

'And it isn't just dirt, if I'm not mistaken.'

Farrell glanced down at his ruined shirt, vest and pants, resisting the temptation to point out that their condition had scarcely been much better even before this morning's encounter. He doffed his battered hat in acknowledgement of her orders and they parted company.

Wes Ferguson looked up from his desk as a tap on the open door of his study revealed Frank McCoy.

'OK if I pay the hands, Mr Ferguson?'

'That branding nearly done?'

'Another couple of hours, I reckon.'

Ferguson glanced at the grandfather clock in the corner and grunted.

'Taken their time over it, haven't they?'

'Done the best we can with a man short.'

'A man short? Well, I ain't payin' no malingerer—'

'There's nobody sick, sir,' McCoy interrupted. 'We've been working without Farrell, remember?'

'What? Oh, yes.'

Ferguson leant back in his chair and fixed his eyes sharply on McCoy.

'He makes that kind of difference, does he?'

McCoy's reply was curt. 'He's good with a rope.'

'And with a horse, I hear from my daughter. She said she watched him cutting out steers the other afternoon like a circus professional.'

McCoy inclined his head in the faintest acknowledgement of this observation, but made no comment.

'Good to know he's shaping up. Hands are two a penny, but good ones – the ones that save you time and money – aren't so easy to come by.'

'No sir.'

There was silence for a moment as if Ferguson were waiting for some sort of positive comment from McCoy, but when the foreman remained mute Ferguson rose, walked over to a cabinet beside his desk, unlocked it and produced a cash-box. He set the box on his desk, opened it and drew out an arrangement of dockets and greenbacks. These he placed in a cloth bag which he passed to McCoy.

'Pay 'em when the work's finished this afternoon. I ain't having nobody sliding off into town with the job half done – however long it takes.'

'No sir.'

Ferguson grunted again.

'I suppose you'll be going into town yourself tonight?'

41

'If that's all right with you.'

'No reason why not. See you keep the boys out of any trouble. And make sure nobody rides back alone. Pacification or no pacification, still too many goddam stray Apaches around for my liking.'

Taking this as a dismissal McCoy turned, clapped on his hat and made his way out across the stone flagged floor of the living-room. As he reached the front door Hetty Ferguson emerged from the dining-room with a duster in her hand.

'Oh, it's you, Frank. Thought I heard the sound of boots. You haven't been messing up the floor, I hope. Maid's only just finished polishing.'

McCoy snatched off his hat and with reddening face glanced down at his scuffed footwear.

'Sorry, Miss Hetty. I had to see your father. But I remembered to wipe my boots.'

'Just teasing.'

Hetty turned and walked back into the dining-room to resume her dusting.

'I . . . er. . . .' McCoy, who had half-followed her in to the room, gave a cough of embarrassment as Hetty spun round with surprise.

'I . . . er . . . was just goin' to ask . . .'

Hetty squinted at him in some puzzlement.

'Ask what, Frank?'

'Well . . . seeing as I'm going into town later I thought I'd ask if there's anything you needed. I could easil—'

'That's very kind of you, Frank, but I'll be making a trip with Pa next week. There's no necessity for you to bother yourself.'

'Ain't no bother, Miss Hetty.' McCoy advanced a step towards her. 'Any time you wants any small service you've only got to ask.'

'Sure.'

There was a perceptible note of discomfort in her voice. McCoy's lean figure was obstructing her passage round the dining-room table. He transferred his hat to the hand that was holding the pay-bag and tentatively stretched out his free hand to touch the sleeve of her dress.

'I mean . . . any service,' he breathed softly. Then he repeated, 'You only gotta ask.'

Hetty clicked her tongue and brushed away his hand with an impatient flick of her duster.

'I heard you the first time Frank – and I already said there isn't anything you can do for me. Now you skedaddle out of here. Pa'll be hollering for his dinner in just two minutes.'

'All right.' McCoy's response was gruff. 'Maybe. . . .'

But his voice trailed off as Hetty turned her back and retreated towards the kitchen. McCoy clamped his hat to his head and strode out. Squinting in the bright early afternoon sunlight he glanced across the yard to where Farrell, having just returned from his visit to town, was unhitching the buckboard. McCoy stood impassively on the porch as Farrell left the wagon and approached the house. As Farrell climbed the steps to the porch McCoy made no move to get out of his way.

'Just where do you think you're going?' he asked, with a jerk of his head.

'Boss asked me to report to him when I got back,' said Farrell, pausing with one foot on the step below the foreman. McCoy reached out and spun Farrell round to face the way he had come.

'You can report to me, and I'll report to the boss,' said McCoy. 'I already told you, you got no business here.'

Unbalanced by McCoy's manoeuvre Farrell stumbled back down the steps with the foreman's hand still on his shoulder.

'Hey, take it easy will you? I was given a job to do and I

43

done it. What's the problem?' Farrell righted himself and turned to face McCoy, who had now joined him at the bottom of the steps.

'Yeah,' said McCoy, ignoring the question. 'And I'm sure you did it real well as usual. Like showing off to Miss Hetty with your fancy horsework.'

'What?' asked Farrell in genuine bewilderment.

'Don't play games with me, mister. I already gave you one warning about trespassing on my territory. Next time I won't be so gentle.' McCoy flicked insolently at his chest with thumb and finger. He chuckled with satisfaction as he noted Farrell's fists clenching.

'Go on. Take a swipe – you owe me one, after all.'

Farrell stared at McCoy's leering features but remained doggedly immobile, ignoring the provocation.

'I just said I got a report to make. You gonna let me make it, or are we going to stand around here all afternoon?'

'All right,' said McCoy, after a pause, and with evident disappointment in his voice at Farrell's refusal to rise to the bait. 'Report.'

Farrell gave him an edited version of events, omitting his role in intercepting the attempted theft of Beth Carney's cash.

'So that's it,' said McCoy, when Farrell had finished. 'Now get your hide over to the corral. We saved you plenty of work.'

Farrell made his way across the yard and out to where the other hands were occupied with the young steers that had been rounded up the previous day. A pungent smell of burning charcoal and singed cattlehide wafted across to his nostrils. He wrinkled his nose in distaste. Of all activities on the ranch this was his least favourite: dirty, tiring and smelly – and comparing very unfavourably with the freedom of riding the range astride a decent horse.

'Hey, Matt,' yelled one of the hands as Farrell strode up. 'We missed ya.'

'I bet you did,' muttered Farrell under his breath.

He skimmed his hat across to land it accurately on one of the upright posts of the corral fence, glanced up at the sun, stripped off his vest, and prepared to get down to work. It was evidently going to be a long hot afternoon.

In fact, three full hours passed before the last of the steers had been disposed of. McCoy, who had been supervising events from a comfortable perch on the fence, had taken care to ensure that Farrell had been given the worst job of throwing and holding each animal (on the stated grounds that he had had an easy morning) and none of the other hands had dissented from the foreman's division of labour. As Farrell sweated and cursed, his one consolation was the thought of the smart new outfit of clothes he had brought back from town and the satisfaction he was going to get from stripping off his present sweatstained and threadbare rig at the end of the afternoon. He would hand them over for incineration to Lee, a Chinese of indeterminate age who had been employed at the ranch since God-knew-when, who presided with cheerful efficiency over both the cookhouse and the laundry.

When the last animal had been disposed of and the hands had been dismissed Farrell collected his clothing parcels, walked over to the washhouse and treated himself to a long shower under a convenient faucet. The water was ice-cold and it was kind of difficult to achieve a decent lather with only a slice of the roughest kind of laundry soap, but the effect was restorative. So was the sensation of pulling on a decent set of clothes. Unfortunately there was no mirror in which to admire the overall effect, but that could be rectified later in town when he called into the barbershop for a really close shave. In any case, the whistles of approval as he sat down with the other hands for grub at the trestle-table outside the cookhouse indicated that his appearance had definitely been changed for the better. There was an exchange of banter as Lee slapped down the platters and a pile of steaks, and then a contented silence as the hands attacked their food.

'Looks like Matt's dead set to get the prettiest girl in the Goldrush tonight,' remarked one of the men enviously. 'With that dude outfit rest of us ain't gonna stand much chance.'

'Then you'll just have to get there before me,' said Farrell. 'Feel like a race into town?'

'Kind of premature, aren't you?' said a voice at the end of the table.

All eyes turned towards McCoy, who had just spoken. Farrell frowned, sensing that he was about to hear bad news.

'What do you mean, premature?'

'You know the house rule,' said McCoy in matter-of-fact tones. 'At least one hand has to stay behind in case of trouble.'

'Yeah, but I—'

'Yeah, but you already had your trip into town. And by the looks of them clothes you used the boss's time real well. Seems only fitting you should stay back and let others have their turn. Ain't that right, boys?'

McCoy surveyed the row of heads along either side of the table for confirmation of his decision. Farrell's companions kept their eyes down on their plates. They were all aware that Farrell had stayed behind the previous Saturday and that he had earned his night off, but such was their fear of McCoy that nobody was prepared to speak up in his defence.

Farrell looked sullenly down the table at the implacable features of the foreman.

'Yes, but I . . .' he began again. And then, aware of the

hopelessness of the situation, he slammed his knife down on the table and strode away to the bunkhouse. McCoy pointed to the half-eaten steak on Farrell's plate.

'Pass it along, boys. Shame to waste good food.'

FOUR

Beth Carney tweaked back the lace curtain as a rumble of wheels and the snorting of horses resounded up from Main Street through her bedroom window at the Goldrush saloon.

'About time.'

She checked her appearance in the dressing-table mirror, drew her mantilla over her head and made her way quickly downstairs into the fading light of the early evening. The stage had drawn in at the Overland office which was conveniently just a few doors along from her newly acquired premises. She noted with approval that her specially liveried young bell-boy, who was part of the carefully planned accoutrements of the Goldrush hotel, had already scurried along to assist with the unloading of the passengers. The general idea was to ensure that any traveller intending to overnight would be snapped up by the Goldrush before he or she could patronize any of the other lesser competing establishments. Beth stepped gingerly round the cases and packages that were being thrown, none too carefully, down from the roof of the coach, and addressed herself to the men up front.

'Thought you were due in at midday.'

'Hi, Mizz Carney,' grunted the driver. 'Bust a wheel just out of Tucson and had to turn back. Then we was given the run-around by some Apaches five miles out of town.'

Beth raised a sceptical eyebrow.

'Don't see no arrows sticking in you.'

'Well,' conceded the driver, 'wasn't exactly an attack – more likely just a hunting party. But they sure make you feel uncomfortable riding alongside and spooking the horses. Anyway,' he continued, pointing back at the freshly painted façade of the new hotel, 'reckon we've done you a good turn as far as business is concerned. We ain't going any further tonight, so I guess you got a wagonload of customers.'

Beth gave a grunt of satisfaction, and broke away to attend to the half-dozen dusty and irritable passengers who were standing beside the vehicle trying to regain control of their personal possessions. Satisfied that none of them was in a fit state to cast about looking for lodgings elsewhere than at the hotel which was right in front of their noses, and that the bell-boy, who had been carefully selected and rehearsed from a large assortment of anxious applicants, had matters well in hand with a nice line in sales patter, she made her way to the hotel foyer to supervise the reception of her guests.

'Looks like we're gonna have a full house tonight,' she remarked to the young man who was standing behind the mahogany reception desk.

'Everything set?'

'Sure thing, ma'am.' He grinned.

'Care to try the bell?' He pointed to the impressive brass bell standing next to the registration book.

'Nope. Tried it this morning.'

Beth stood discreetly to one side as the passengers began to file into the foyer. There were four gentlemen and two ladies, none of whom seemed to have found the journey, or the prospect of an unanticipated stay in Pinedale Fork, remotely agreeable. Beth remained in her position, offering a kind but discreet word to the ladies, and ensuring that the processes of registration and room allocation went according to plan. The last of the passengers to sign the book was a middle-aged man who had the world-weary look of a commercial traveller.

'Whole day to travel twenty miles,' he remarked sourly to Beth as he put down the pen. 'Time this territory got itself organized. Broken wheels, Injun escorts . . .'

'We're trying,' said Beth with an ironic glance towards the receptionist. 'Perhaps you'd care to wet your whistle at the bar when you've unpacked?' She indicated the door at the far end of the foyer which led to the passage she had had constructed connecting directly into the saloon. 'One of our hostesses will be glad to take care of you.'

The drummer cocked an eyebrow at her as they exchanged complicit glances.

'Might just do that,' he nodded. 'A little entertainment might not come amiss after a day with only this for reading matter.' He threw down a dusty copy of a newspaper on to the counter. 'Here – catch up with the news. I read it three times over already.'

As the bell-boy escorted the man up to his room Beth gave the receptionist a satisfied smile.

'So far, so good.'

She glanced down at the newspaper, but refrained from soiling her hands with it. Letters and newspapers from points east would be unloaded from the coach and available at the mail office later. She preferred her news clean. She was about to turn away when her eye fell on the lead story of the paper, which was lying front page uppermost. She frowned, studied it more closely and then tucked it under her arm, dust and all.

'Call me if you got any problems. I'll be upstairs.'

'Yes, ma'am.'

Beth turned and made her way through the connecting

door into the saloon. The lights were ablaze, the room was filling up with the usual Saturday night crowd, and the piano was rattling away in the corner. She cast an appraising glance around to ensure that the staff were attending to their various duties, and made her way back to her room without speaking to anybody.

Upstairs she closed her door, walked over to the dressing-table and lit the oil-lamp, turning it up bright enough to read by. She sat down, unfolded the newspaper and read the lead story up and down twice. Then she laid the paper to one side and slid open the top drawer of the dressing-table. Rummaging under a carefully folded selection of silk stockings she extracted an envelope and removed the single sheet of folded writing paper it contained. Tilting the paper towards the lamp she scanned the scrawled contents with an occasional glance back at the newspaper as if for verification of what she was reading. Then she refolded the paper, put it back in its envelope and replaced it in the drawer.

'So that's it,' she muttered, drumming her fingers on the table.

For a minute or two she sat staring out of the window as the shadows fell over Main Street beneath her, and the lights in the windows of the commercial premises in either direction began to shine on the sidewalks. Then she rose from her chair and made her way down to the street again, using the backstairs so that her exit would be unobserved.

This time she turned her steps in the opposite direction, crossing Main Street and walking along the boardwalk until she came to Jade Finch's office. The blinds were drawn, but chinks of light around the edges indicated that the office was occupied. Beth tapped on the door, turned the handle and slipped inside.

Finch was sitting at his desk sifting through a pouch of

mail which had obviously just arrived on the stage. He looked up.

'Figured I might find you at home,' said Beth, taking a seat without being asked.

'Saturday night,' said Finch. 'Best night of the week for business. I like to be where people can find me. You got trouble?'

Beth shook her head. 'Not at the Goldrush. Too early.'

'If it's about your brother, I finished my inspection of the . . . er . . . body. I mean, if you want to make the funeral . . .'

Beth put up her hand. 'Time enough for that. I'm sure Joe Doyle's already lining out his most expensive coffin, knowing I'll be footin' the bill.'

There was silence for a moment and then Beth leant forward.

'You done any figuring about all this?'

Finch stroked his chin.

'Some,' he said, non-committally. 'Thought I might have young Farrell in and give him a real grilling this time. Can't exclude the possibility that he knows more than he was letting on. Just a pity that knives like this . . . (he waved his hand in the direction of the murder weapon which was still lying in its wrapping on his desk) . . . are two a dime in this part of the world. Every cowpoke in the territory has one – or more.'

'Yeah,' said Beth, her voice dry with suppressed tension. 'Well, it's about the knife that I came to see you. I think I know who it belongs to.'

Matt Farrell lay stretched out on his quilt in the bunkhouse moodily contemplating the smoke-blackened roof beams above him. The bustle and joshing of the other hands as they prepared for their foray into the delights of Pinedale Fork had gradually subsided, leaving him to contemplate the prospect of several long, solitary hours ahead. Even the solace of an early turn-in was forbidden as it was a ranch rule that the duty hand had to remain alert until the main body of men returned.

His first thought on throwing himself down on the bed had been to tell McCoy what to do with his job, saddle his horse and ride out. The fifty dollars from Beth Carney, which were even now burning a hole in his pocket, would provide a comfortable cushion until he found another job, and in any case experienced hands with his abilities were always in demand. Starvation would not threaten. But as his temper cooled, he found himself increasingly disinclined to give McCoy a painless victory by marching cravenly off his cabbage patch. That the foreman wanted him out was as clear as daylight, but the reason for his sudden hostility was still difficult for Farrell to grasp. What on earth had he meant by his reference to Farrell showing off in front of Miss Hetty?

Farrell cast his mind back to the incident when she had encountered him out on the range cutting out steers, but he had certainly not been trying to impress – indeed he had been totally unaware of her presence until she rode up to him. And in any case, he had only been doing a mundane job. Miss Hetty herself as a rancher's daughter was no slouch in the saddle, so it was unlikely that she would have seen Farrell's performance as anything but professional routine. So what on earth was McCoy worried about? And anyway . . . he didn't feel like job hunting. Until yesterday he had been quietly satisfied with his billet at Ferguson's. Five dollars a week was as much as he could expect anywhere, the food and living conditions were OK, and the ranch was an easy ride to the diversions of Pinedale Fork.

Farrell had already made up his mind that after years of drifting he wouldn't move again unless he could get the foreman's job that his experience and capabilities entitled him to, and now, as a matter of self-respect, he wasn't going to quit without some sort of settling of accounts with McCoy. How this was to be achieved wasn't yet clear, but time would no doubt provide an answer. He was just rehearsing in his mind the various unpleasant snares that he might set for his antagonist when his thought processes were interrupted by the sound of boots approaching the bunkhouse.

The door was thrown open abruptly and Farrell turned his head to see the figure of Jim Lester stumping towards him.

'Hi, Matt. Feelin' sorry for yourself?'

Farrell ignored the question and resumed his examination of the ceiling. As Lester sat down heavily on the adjacent bed Farrell spoke without looking at him.

'Aren't you supposed to be in town? I thought I heard you all ride off.'

'Nope,' said Lester. 'Told McCoy I wanted a quiet night in and said I'd swap with you.'

Farrell frowned. 'You did what?'

'Said I'd change places with you – you got cloth ears or somethin'?'

'Yeah, I heard you,' said Farrell, levering himself up into a sitting position. 'But there ain't no call for you to be making any sacrifices just because McCoy and I are having a spat. I can sort out my own problems.'

Lester contemplated him in silence for a moment before replying.

'Guess you're sore because none of us spoke up for you at the table.'

'Yeah . . . well . . . would that surprise you any?'

Lester spat on the floor and chuckled.

'Nope. We didn't exactly cover ourselves with glory. But see here, Matt. You know how it is. This is a decent crib

54

and the men want their jobs. You know they can't step out of line with McCoy. Maybe all right for you youngsters, but where am I goin' to get another job at my age? It's not that they didn't feel for you. Hell, even if you only been here a few months or so they know you're the best hand in the outfit.'

'All right,' said Farrell. His tone was softer, mollified by the unexpected, and unprecedented, compliment. 'So how come you finally screwed up your courage to do some negotiating?'

'No trouble at all. Frank and I go back a long way, and he owes me a few favours. Weren't no point picking him up in front of the other men, because he'd have gone as prickly as a cactus and dug his heels in like the mule-headed son-of-a-bitch he is. Just waited my moment to get him alone and tell him I was staying behind anyway.'

'Oh.' Farrell chewed his lip. 'But look, you really don't have to stay back just to help me out of a hole. I already said I could fight my own battles.'

'Sure. And I sure don't know what's up between you and Frank. Seemed to me you were just getting along fine. But I really don't care about goin' into town tonight to blow a week's pay on booze and poker. Figure at my age I ought to be acting with a little more decorum – and saving my pay for my old age. So far I ain't got nothing put by. So you get your butt out of that there bunk and put on those fancy boots you just acquired for yourself.'

Farrell smiled, but shook his head.

'Thanks, Jim. But it won't work. You know the rule – I can't ride out alone. McCoy would bust my hide for that, and so would the old man if he found out.'

'Alone, fiddle-de-dee. Charlie Wilson held back so as to ride with you. He's outside with your horse right now. So git before I change my mind and go with him.'

Farrell swung his legs on to the floor with alacrity, holding out his hand to Lester while inwardly regretting the unkind thoughts he had frequently harboured about the old man's often senile performance out on the range.

'Kind of reassuring to know I got friends,' he said as they shook hands.

'Aw shucks. You should have knowed that without being told.'

Farrell and Wilson made short work of the ride into town: even at night the trail was well marked and easy to follow, and the lights of Pinedale Fork were clearly visible from more than a mile out. They rode in silence – Wilson because he was a man of few words anyway, and Farrell because he was mulling over an idea that had come to him as a result of something Jim Lester had said back in the bunkhouse.

Once in town they separated: Wilson went straight to the nearest saloon, Farrell to the barbershop where he spent a pleasant half-hour catching up with the local news – most of it concerning the discovery of Beth Carney's defunct brother. Then, massaging his newly scraped chin with satisfaction, he made his way along to the Goldrush. The sounds of the usual Saturday night revelries were clearly audible a hundred yards away, and the lights from the saloon's plate-glass windows shone bright on the boardwalk in either direction and clear across the street.

He hitched his horse and thrust his way through the swing-doors. Inside, the cacophony of sounds was almost painful after the relative quietness of Main Street. At one end of the long saloon a group of cowhands were clustered around the bar evidently intent on drinking themselves into oblivion; to the rear three or four card-tables were already in operation; and at the far end the first of the twice-nightly burlesque shows was just getting into its stride.

Farrell threaded his way through the tables, exchanging

greetings with a few familiar faces, until he fetched up at the end of the long bar furthest away from the revellers, and perched himself on a stool.

'Whiskey,' he ordered.

The bartender had scarcely had time to pour his drink when one of Beth Carney's prettiest sylphs slipped on to the adjacent stool.

'Hi, handsome. Care to buy a girl a drink?'

Farrell recognized Maisie, whose company he had enjoyed on other occasions. 'Hi. Sure. Whaddya havin'?'

'Champagne.'

The reply was both instantaneous and institutionally *de rigueur*. Farrell shrugged with good humour. The Goldrush's prices were fixed at levels calculated not to break the average cowpoke's wallet – hence its commercial success – and with fifty dollars in his pocket he was effectively a millionaire for the night. The drink was served, and as Maisie raised her glass in a friendly toast her fingers slid enticingly along the inside of his thigh.

'You lookin' for company tonight, Matt? Heard tell as how you came into money. . . .'

Trust Pinedale Fork to circulate private and personal information like wildfire, he thought, as Maisie's fingers lingered on his knee and beads of perspiration suddenly burst out on his forehead.

'Kinda hot in here, ain't it?' he commented, taking off his hat and laying it on the counter.

'Hadn't noticed.'

Farrell glanced down at her décolletage. Her blue-satin gown was real pretty, but it seemed to end quite abruptly before reaching her shoulders.

'Maybe you should try wearing a bit more clothing.'

Maisie giggled. 'Mizz Carney likes us to show a bit of titty-fa-la. You aiming to lodge a complaint?' Her hand tightened on his knee.

The whiskey was coursing through his system like a purgative, easing away all the tensions of the day, and the prospect of a closer encounter with this particular siren was powerfully enticing. But he had set an entirely different objective for himself on the ride into town, and refused to be distracted.

'Sorry, honey. Nothing personal, but I got other business tonight.'

As a pout of disappointment crossed her face Farrell hastily reached into his pocket and extracted a couple of greenbacks.

'Here,' he said, pressing the notes discreetly into her hand. 'Go have yourself a good time anyway.'

As the girl slipped away in search of another prospect Farrell downed the remainder of his drink, stood up, walked discreetly over to a door alongside the bar, and tapped softly. There was a pause as he was presumably surveyed from the other side of what he knew to be a one-way glass panel, and then a click as Beth Carney opened her office door.

'Why, Matt. Heard you wasn't comin' into town tonight.'

'Things changed.'

'Good. Swell outfit you got yourself there. Would have been kind of a pity to waste it.'

Beth stepped back slightly to admire Farrell's new accoutrements.

'Well, you have yourself a good time tonight, you hear? I gotta new girl, name of—'

Farrell put out his hand to interrupt the sales pitch.

'Sorry. I was fixin' to play a little cards.'

'Oh. Well, help yourself.' She gestured behind him towards the baize covered tables where various poker-games were already in progress.

Farrell cleared his throat.

58

'Er, as a matter of fact I had something a bit better in mind than them dime ante games. Seeing as how I suddenly came into money, if you know what I mean.'

Beth stared at him and then laughed.

'Sure you're strong enough for the big boys?'

Farrell nodded.

'Quite sure. So how about it? Do I qualify?'

Beth pursed her lips.

'All right.'

She closed the office and led Farrell across the room to another door marked PRIVATE – NO ADMITTANCE EXCEPT BY INVITATION. Farrell took a deep breath as she ushered him inside. It had been Lester's passing reference to not spending his pay on booze and poker that had set his mind working on the theme of cards as a means of resolving his current personal difficulties. The small-scale front of house poker-games had been a bread-and-butter part of his Saturday nights here for many months, but with fifty bucks in his pocket he had been given an unconstrained opportunity to exercise his skills at a higher level. The private room housed a much bigger game reserved for the more prosperous local tradespeople and senior cattlemen. And as Farrell peered inside through the haze of tobacco smoke he saw with satisfaction that, as anticipated, his quarry was all set up. McCoy was sitting facing him with a pile of chips all ready to be plundered.

FIVE

The card-table was a large circular baize-covered affair placed under a low green-shaded chandelier. There were six men seated at the table concentrating on the cards in front of them. Nobody had looked up as the door opened.

'New player, Pete. Give him chips.'

At the sound of Beth's voice one or two heads turned with mild curiosity to inspect the newcomer. McCoy squinted through the cigar smoke and recognized Farrell. His protest was loud and sharp.

'Hey. What's going on? This is a fifty-buck buy-in game. Since when did cowpokes—'

'Mr Farrell's good for the buy-in,' said Beth, cutting him off in mid-tirade. 'And if you object to his company there are tables outside.'

'Sit down, cowboy,' said Pete Swallow, another of Beth's aged retainers, turning to Farrell with an encouraging smile. He indicated a space to his right.

'Fifty,' said Farrell, reaching in to his shirt pocket and producing a roll of greenbacks. Swallow reached across and exchanged the cash for a stack of chips extracted from a rack in front him.

'Guess you know the rules, but I'll just repeat them. Fifty cents ante, dollar minimum bet before the draw, two bucks min after the draw and pot limit maximum. Jacks or better to open. House rake dime in the dollar up to five bucks. That exciting enough for you?'

Farrell nodded. He was familiar with the structure of the game although he had never participated before. The relatively high ante was designed to encourage action, and although the level of the minimum bets was set deceptively low, the pot limit rule allowed raises to proceed exponentially if players felt like getting competitive. He eased himself into his chair and glanced around the table. There were five other active players. Swallow was employed solely as dealer by the house and was responsible for the conduct of the game and the cutting of the house rake from each pot. A marker, consisting of a silver dollar, rotated clockwise from player to player with each hand indicating the notional dealer and determining the order of betting. McCoy, of course, was a familiar face; of the others Farrell recognized Doyle, the timber merchant, Doc Wilson, and the proprietor of the general merchandise stores, Peake. The other two, Farrell learnt, were Murchison and Bredin, two small time ranchers from the other side of town.

'Ante up, gentlemen,' said Swallow gathering in the cards from the previous deal and executing an accomplished riffle. As Beth withdrew, Farrell picked up the cards that had been expertly skimmed across the baize and studied his first hand. He had been a poker-player ever since his teens and, like most young men, had found the learning process expensive. But with greater maturity had come experience and a genuine feel for the probabilities and psychology of the game, so that for the last two years or so he had been able to sit at small-time games in the bunkhouse or the saloon and enjoy more winning sessions than losing ones.

One early lesson he had mastered was that in games where you were a fresh face – and therefore an unknown quantity – it paid to set up a smokescreen around your true ability as soon as you sat down. If accomplished successfully it could have the effect of wrongfooting your opponents for the rest of the session. So the first task he had set himself tonight would not be to win a hand, but to lose it. There were times, Farrell reflected, as he fingered his cards, when this was a greater art form than winning – at least if you were to do it cheaply and effectively. But for the moment there was nothing to tax his ingenuity: the cards were a set of unrelated duds, and although the pot had been opened ahead of him the hand was an automatic fold. As were the next two. Farrell began to feel a prickle of unease. At fifty cents a hand, each round was costing three dollars, so to sit folding was not an option if he wanted to avoid the steady erosion of his capital.

'You planning to join us in any of these pots?' enquired Doyle solicitously, to an accompaniment of approving chuckles around the table. 'Come on in, the water's just fine.'

Farrell affected what he hoped was a nervous smile and squeezed his cards gingerly, raising them just an inch or so from the baize. He was relieved to see a pair of red queens simpering up at him from amongst the otherwise undistinguished assortment.

'Your call, Mr Farrell,' said Pete, indicating the silver dollar which showed that Doyle, to Farrell's immediate right was the notional dealer, and that Farrell, therefore, was first to speak.

'What? Oh, sure. Guess I'd better open, as Mr Doyle's so keen to win my money.'

Farrell slid a dollar chip forward, hoping that he was about to make a good long-term investment. Although the queens qualified him to open the pot, in first position with all the other players yet to speak, only a real palooka or total greenhorn would make such a dumb move – the hand was far too weak to be playable even in a relatively loose game as this was. Which made it ideal for his present purpose. Wilson and Doyle called, evidently taking his bet at face value, but to Farrell's relief neither of them raised. Phew!

'How many?'

'Two,' said Farrell, keeping the queens with a useless four of spades kicker and discarding his other rags.

Wilson to his left took one card, and Doyle took three. Scooping up his two replacements Farrell was delighted to see that neither of them improved his hand. In his current manoeuvre of inverted priorities three queens or even two pair would have been something of a setback. The pot now stood at six dollars, so trying to act with the confidence of one who has just made a pat hand, he bet the pot, hoping that none of the other players would notice the slight tremble in his hand. Wilson, who had presumably been drawing to a four-card straight or draw, grunted, squinted sideways at Farrell and then back at his cards. There was a pause as he considered what to do. Presumably not having made his hand, he was evidently suspicious that Farrell was trying some sort of smart play. But with Doyle still to act behind him, it would have been an expensive risk to bet the pot back at Farrell just to expose his bluff and then get beaten by whatever Doyle was holding. He folded.

As Farrell had hoped, Doyle, with a substantial pile of chips in front of him, was not intimidated, but was a careful enough player not to raise him back.

'Best keep you honest, cowboy,' he muttered as he called Farrell's bet.

Farrell proudly spread his hand.

'Pair of queens,' announced Swallow, turning to Doyle.

'Nice hand,' said Doyle in a tone that for a second suggested to Farrell that he might have pulled off the unexpected and unintended feat of actually winning. 'But not quite nice enough.'

He turned over his hand to reveal kings over fives.

'Aw, shucks,' said Farrell in apparent surprise and disappointment. The hand had cost him seven bucks fifty – which was a significant slice of his original buy-in – but he hoped that it would provide good advertising for false credentials. The other players would take due note that they were only up against a patsy who thought you could open under the gun with nothing better than queens, and downrate his play accordingly. From now on he could guarantee that every sizeable bet he made would be called. If they were really smart they would also have noted, as Farrell had, that Doyle had revealed himself as an unsound player: to come in with just kings against an opening bet in first position was a move in defiance of all probabilities. Farrell riffled his chips with apparent discomfiture, covertly noting significant glances being exchanged around the table, and an ironic smirk plastered across McCoy's face. So far, so good.

For the next half-hour or so Farrell concentrated on recovering his investment and building a modest stack of profits, seeking no dramatic confrontations but content to notch up intermittent apparently lucky wins. He had also noticed over the years that your strike rate seemed to improve if you concentrated your attention on one particular opponent at a time as a target – preferably the weakest player if you could identify him, or the one with the least chips. McCoy was his real prey tonight, but for the moment he directed his attention to Doyle, who seemed to be playing with scant respect for the mathematics of the game, possibly because the money didn't mean that much to him: by all accounts the timber business was thriving, not to mention the monopoly he enjoyed as the town's sole disposer of the local deceased. Only when Farrell had doubled his stack and Doyle had twice been forced to rebuy chips, did he switch the direction of his attack.

McCoy rarely deigned to join in the regular bunkhouse sessions back at the ranch, but from his occasional cameo appearances Farrell had marked him down as a solid player with just enough aggression to ensure respect. The undermining of McCoy's self-belief would have to be carefully handled, and the first step in the demolition process came when Farrell found himself in late position holding a pair of kings. As the other players ahead of him folded, Farrell bet the pot in a standard positional ploy to steal the antes. McCoy, to his left, and notional dealer, reached for his chips.

'Stealing again, cowboy?' he sneered, and raised the pot back at him.

Farrell cursed his own inattention and the fate that had led him to try a routine steal – or to be more precise, semi-steal – just when McCoy had been dealt (presumably) a pair of aces. But to fold at this point would be craven, even though it was now going to cost him six dollars – more than a week's pay, he reflected – to draw to a hand that was clearly the underdog. Sensing that his whole strategy was in danger of running off the rails he pushed his chips forward without any trace of hesitation.

'Call.'

'How many?' enquired the dealer, preparing for the draw.

This time Farrell allowed himself a moment for reflection. The only positive feature of the situation was that one of his unmatched cards was an ace. In the ordinary course of events he might have considered retaining it with the kings as a kicker. But if his hypothesis that McCoy was holding aces was correct, then his own ace was useless and could be safely discarded. What was more, it reduced McCoy's chances of improving his hand.

'Three,' said Farrell, making his discards.

When McCoy also drew three Farrell breathed a faint

65

sigh of relief. At least the remote possibility that McCoy
had originally been dealt a pat flush or straight was now
ruled out. Farrell peeked at his replacement cards and
discovered that he had collected a pair of eights to give
him kings up. It could have been worse. So now he sat
back for a moment to consider whether to bet or check.
This, he reflected, was one of the real bread-and-butter
situations that made poker the absorbing game it was. Pat
hands like straights and flushes – which in his case only
seemed to turn up at sadly infrequent intervals – generally
tended to play themselves. But making two pair and being
in the disadvantageous situation of having to speak first
against an opponent who had made a similar draw was a
real test of judgement. Because, of course, there was no
right answer. Everything depended on the state of the
game and what you knew about your opponent. And yet if
you could make accurate decisions – doing, say, the right
thing two out of three times – that was where the steady
profits were to be made.

In a way, it sort of represented the card-table equivalent
of knowing when, and in what circumstances, to take on
an opponent in a bare-knuckle fight. You had to consider
the man *and* the situation. And now, as he studied his
cards, and absent-mindedly riffled his chips with his free
hand, Farrell pondered what he knew about McCoy's playing style. Farrell felt that he could safely discount the
remote possibility that McCoy had drawn the case ace to
give him three of a kind. So the question was, had he
drawn another pair? McCoy maintained an inscrutable
face, and had no other tells or mannerisms which would
have given Farrell any clue as to whether he had improved
his hand or not. So now it was an exercise in logic.

One conclusion which was immediately obvious was
that if Farrell checked, McCoy would be certain to bet –
and bet the pot. Either McCoy had made his hand, or

would read Farrell's check as weakness and confirmation of his stated suspicion that Farrell had only been trying to steal the antes – so he would be sure to come out shooting. In which case, concluded Farrell, his only available strategy was to come out betting himself. And he could be sure of two things. Firstly, even if McCoy hadn't improved his hand he would be certain to call – Farrell's previous loose play had already ensured that response. Secondly, he knew from McCoy's playing style that he was too savvy to raise as a bluff against a loose player. If he raised, Farrell could fold, in the certain knowledge that he had been beaten. It would hurt and humiliate, but it would save money. All that was unclear was whether McCoy had defied the odds and drawn a pair to go with his aces, and there was only one way to find out. There were now eighteen dollars in the centre of the table. Farrell methodically counted out the requisite number of chips and bet the pot.

'Smart move for a pocket-picker,' said McCoy. His hand moved towards his chips, as Farrell tried to feign indifference to his response. After a momentary hesitation which seemed like an eternity McCoy flicked just eighteen dollars across the table.

'Call.'

Farrell wondered whether his relieved exhalation of breath had been audible across the table. Certain that he had won, he spread his cards on the baize with a provocative victory rip.

'Nice hand for a rustler,' remarked Doc Wilson with a twinkle in his eye.

McCoy stared at the cards with an expression of disgust mixed with disbelief. Although as the player who had called he could have mucked his cards without exposing them and simply conceded the pot, he threw his hand face up on the table. As Farrell had surmised, he had been holding two aces which he had failed to improve.

'Unlucky son-of-a-bitch, Frank,' remarked Bredin. 'You had him licked up to the draw.'

'Yeah,' snarled McCoy. He turned to Farrell who was calmly stacking his winnings.

'You got lucky, cowboy. Next time you make a dumb play like that I'll bust your ass.' Farrell stared across at him with wide-eyed innocence, aware that he had, indeed, fallen on his feet against the odds.

'Well,' he remarked in a tone which adroitly combined innocence with insolence, 'not all trappers wear fur hats.'

McCoy shoved back his chair in an angry gesture.

'What kind of cheapskate crack is that, junior? You got something against my play?'

'Not at all,' said Farrell, caressing the additional stack of chips that had now been joined to his playing capital. 'I can't wait to get more of it.'

As McCoy made to rise from his chair, Bredin laid a restraining hand on his arm. 'Cool it, Frank. You know Beth likes the game to stay quiet.'

'You guys from Ferguson's sure play hard,' remarked Peake. 'That what it's always like up there?'

'Ain't nobody's business but ours,' said McCoy, settling back into his chair. 'I just don't like sassy cowhands.' He turned to Pete Swallow. 'Deal for chris'sake, will ya.'

'Sure thing,' said Swallow. 'As soon as you've ante'd.'

McCoy stared down at his depleted stack and flicked a chip across the baize with such venom that it almost skidded off the far side of the table. Farrell observed this display of spleen with quiet satisfaction. The hand had only resulted in a modest dent in McCoy's chips, but he knew that the psychological damage would be enormous. From now on McCoy would find him impossible to read and impossible to leave unchallenged. The process of erosion would be slow but inexorable. All Farrell had to do was sit back and watch him destroy himself.

It took a couple of hours for McCoy's stack to dwindle to the point where he needed to stage a real coup in order to have any hope of staying in the game. He had taken no opportunity of bringing out more cash, so Farrell assumed that the residual collection of chips in front of him represented his total resources. Any one of the other players might have bust McCoy out at this point but Farrell was happy to do the job for them. McCoy had pulled the old trick of betting the pot before the draw and then standing pat. With just the two of them in contest Farrell, who had failed to improve on the pair of aces he had started with, studied McCoy's remaining chips and contemptuously counted out exactly enough to set him all-in. There was a possibility that McCoy might have actually been dealt a flush or straight or was trying a semi-bluff with pat triplets, but with no chance of a re-raise Farrell was prepared to risk it. McCoy called the bet with a distracted expression on his face and was halfway out of his chair even before Farrell could turn over his cards.

'I quit,' said McCoy, mucking his cards, his voice thick with rage. 'Wrong kind of company in here tonight.'

Doyle turned to Farrell.

'That all you have to do to win? Seems to me the game got easier.'

'Yeah,' grinned Farrell. 'Or maybe it's just because I been living right.'

'Well, you make sure you stay living, mister,' snarled McCoy, grabbing his hat. As the door slammed behind him Bredin leant over to Farrell.

'You boys share a bedroom back at the ranch?'

The enquiry provoked an outburst of ironic laughter from the rest of the company, but as Farrell joined in the hilarity he found himself reviewing both his immediate and long-term prospects. As far as he could make out, McCoy had lost well over a hundred dollars – the equivalent of at least two months' pay – much of it to Farrell. So life on the ranch was about to become purgatory. In fact, he found himself wondering whether he had just succeeded in shooting himself in the foot. He played on without much enthusiasm, and was just wondering what excuse to make to back out, when there was a tap at the door and one of the bartenders entered.

'Sorry to intrude gentlemen, but there's a message for Doc Wilson. He's needed at his surgery.'

Wilson looked up.

'Tarnation. Hope that don't mean old Zach's taken a turn for the worst. I had him laying up on my best couch.'

He pushed his chips towards the dealer.

'Cash me out. Sorry to break up the party, gentlemen, but duty calls.'

He collected his cash, clamped on his hat, and made his way out. With the game now down by two players, Farrell was able to mutter something about not liking to play short-handed and seize the excuse to cash out and make his own exit to the saloon.

It was nearing midnight and the Saturday night high-jinks at the Goldrush were at full swing. Farrell ensconced himself at the bar, ordered a drink and peered around to see if any of the other hands from the ranch were around. As far as he could make out there were no familiar faces. Perhaps they were at the other end of the room where the midnight show was just getting under way. He was just pouring a beer down his parched throat when he felt a sharp prod in his back. He turned to find Clem Parker, one of the sheriff's assistants, standing behind him. Farrell frowned.

'Somethin' wrong?'

'Just come outside, mister.'

'What?'

'You heard. Put your drink down nice and easy and step outside.'

Farrell was unable to make out from the expression on the man's face whether he had just been given an order or an invitation. Farrell studied his glass for a moment before replying.

'Why in tarnation would I do that?'

'Because the sheriff wants to see you, and he don't like to be kept waiting.'

SIX

Farrell and his escort slipped unobtrusively through the crowd and made their way out into Main Street. There were few people about. Although Farrell recognized the other man from this morning's fracas he still felt uneasy. The summons to see Finch, and its timing, seemed distinctly strange. Almost without thinking Farrell slid his right hand up towards his hip, to reassure himself that his gunbelt and holster were in position in case of trouble. They walked in silence up the street to the sheriff's office. Inside, Farrell found, as he had expected, Finch seated behind his desk. What he had not expected to see, however, was Beth Carney sitting in the armchair she had occupied this morning. Farrell looked from one to the other in some bewilderment.

'Kind of late, isn't it?'

Finch made no reply.

'Thanks, Clem,' he said to Farrell's escort. 'Guess you can skedaddle.'

As the other man disappeared Finch motioned Farrell to a chair.

'Earlier this evening,' he said, 'Mrs Carney here came to me with some fresh information about her brother. It's taken me a little time to do some necessary verification because the stage was late and this here mass of paper only

72

turned up on my desk a coupla hours ago.'

'Yeah? What has it got to do—'

'Listen a moment. Seems like a couple of *bandidos* pulled a bank job in Tucson a month or so ago. Apparently the authorities grabbed one of them last week on a tip-off. But the other one, identity unknown, had already vamoosed – with the money, presumably.'

'Right,' said Farrell. He frowned. 'But I still don't see—'

'Matt,' said Beth Carney, cutting in, 'the other guy was my brother.'

'Your brother? But how do you know. You said you hadn't seen him in years.'

'Yeah, well that was true. But I wasn't entirely honest when I told the sheriff here about the letter I said Jake had sent me. Sure, he wrote that he was on his way to see me, but he said a bit more than that. He didn't give an address, but the envelope was postmarked Tucson, which made him a good deal closer than I ever thought he was. He also said that he and a partner were in a spot of trouble and he needed somewhere to lie low. That was where I came in, of course.'

There was a pause as Farrell digested this information. Then he leant forward.

'All right. But I still don't see the connection—'

'Neither did I this morning,' Beth interrupted again. 'Until I picked up a copy of that.' She pointed towards Finch's desk, where a copy of the Tucson newspaper was lying, front page uppermost.

'The bank story's slap bang on the front page. It was then I started to put two and two together.'

'But . . .' Farrell frowned again, still not entirely follow- ing the logic of what he was hearing.

'Read the first paragraph,' said Finch, leaning forward to tap the newspaper.

Farrell picked it up, scanned the leading story, and then

dropped the paper back on the desk.

'Oh.' Farrell sat back in surprise. The captured bank robber was named as one Charlie McCoy.

'You sayin' Charlie McCoy and Frank are family?'

'I'm speculating,' grunted Finch. 'As was Mizz Beth when she drew this to my attention earlier this evening. Seems to me the circumstances at least warrant asking the question – I mean, Jake Sibley ending up dead on land where a guy named McCoy just happens to be foreman.'

'Yes, but Frank never mentioned no brother or cousin.'

'So what. Have you ever talked about your family?'

'Guess not.'

Farrell chewed his lip. Finch had a valid point. The unspoken rule on ranches was that nobody asked questions and nobody knew anything about you except what you chose to tell them. Which in most cases wasn't much.

'Anyway,' continued Finch. 'Here's how I figure at least one possibility. Charlie and Jake split up for safety and Jake makes for Pinedale Fork where he knows he can lie up quiet with his obliging sister here. But he's got one errand on the way: to stash the money somewhere safe where it won't be found if he's picked up in Pinedale. So they arrange for him to drop it off with Charlie's local kith and kin. Blood's thicker than water, after all. And Frank's a respectable member of the community. No reason for anyone suspecting him of being associated with a pair of *bandidos*. Frank and Jake meet up by the trail and then things go wrong. Maybe Frank wants a cut, maybe he wants all of it, and quite possibly he doesn't see why Jake should get any of it. Whatever. He kills him and helps himself. The body's left lying somewhere it wouldn't ordinarily be found too quickly. Then you spoil the plan by accidentally finding it, and Beth here caps it by being around when it was ... er ... unveiled. Otherwise it might never have been identified.'

74

Farrell stared at Finch's impassive figure, glanced across to Beth, and then scratched his head in bewilderment.

'Yeah. Nice enough theory. But where's the proof? You don't even know that Frank's got any family like a brother or a cousin. And you've got nothing to prove he did the killing. Nobody saw anything and the knife could have belonged to any cattleman or trail tramp – they're all over the territory.'

Finch nodded in agreement.

'Sure. As to the family, it'll take me a few days to make enquiries, but it shouldn't be difficult.'

'Why don't you come straight out and ask him?'

'And let him know he's a suspect?' asked Finch, with a shake of his head. 'No good giving the game away at this stage. Which is where you come in, of course.'

Farrell, who had been puzzling why he had been rail-roaded over to be privy to the sheriff's theorizing, suddenly found himself jerked into a state of acute alertness.

'Me? What in hell. . . ?'

'Play ball with me a little longer, will you?' continued Finch, with a wave of his hand. 'If I'm right about McCoy the money's got to be somewhere on the ranch. He simply hasn't had time to get rid of it. And for the moment it's even a bit of an embarrassment to him. He can't start spending it, because people would notice. And if he just ran off from a job he's had for I don't know how many years, that would be noticed too. The money's the key to the whole affair. As you say, up to now it's all circumstantial. But find the money on him and it's proof.'

Farrell, with a sinking feeling that he knew exactly what was coming next, made a final attempt to distance himself from the inevitable.

'Hey, now look. I already done my bit. I found the body, I brought it in like a good citizen, I busted Mizz Beth's thief and nearly got my head shot off. Ease up on me, will you?'

But Finch was imperturbable.

'I just need someone on the inside at the ranch who can do a bit of discreet ferreting about without drawing attention to himself. It's no good me simply moseying up there and telling old man Ferguson I'd like to rip his premises apart on the off-chance his foreman's a murderer. Be reasonable.'

Out of patience, and irritated with the sheriff's apparent assumption that he would be a willing catspaw, Farrell stood up. But before he could unleash the torrent of invective that seemed appropriate to the occasion the silence was shattered by the sound of boots running along the boardwalk outside. The door burst open and Clem Parker reappeared.

'Thought ya ought to know, Jade. Zach's just died. Heard it from someone outside Doc Wilson's place.'

'Oh. That's a real shame.' Finch turned to Beth Carney. 'I'm sorry to hear—'

'Yeah,' interrupted Clem. 'But that ain't the half of it. Seems like the news is spreading round town like wildfire and folks don't like what's happened. They're fixin' to come up here and find out what you're going to do about it.'

'Do about it?' grunted Finch, rising to his feet. 'What the hell do they think I'm goin' to do about it? I've already got the kid who did it sitting in a cell back of this office.'

'Sure you have,' said Clem. 'But the way people see it, things has changed. This morning it was a case of attempted robbery. But if Zach's dead as a result of what the kid did to him it's—'

'Manslaughter.'

'Makes it kind of different, don't it?' said Beth pursing her lips.

76

Finch scratched his head and then spoke as if running a few thoughts past himself.

'Of course it alters the picture. I let the boys rough the kid up a bit this morning, but they didn't get much out of him, other than his name, Ben Ashwood, and the fact that he comes from those shanties up the far end of town. I figured he could have a coupla days in a cell with bread and water and then we'd boot him out of town. But of course if it's manslaughter we've got to bring charges. Damn the kid – so much tarnation paperwork.'

Parker shook his head in dissent.

'Ain't gonna be a question of paperwork. That's the point. Zach was a real popular old-timer and folks want quick justice. You hear that. . . ?'

Clem opened the office door a crack to allow the sound of distant baying and trampling of feet to penetrate. Finch spat out a disgusted oath.

'Lock the door, Clem. Danged if I'm taking orders from any collection of late-night drunks.'

The key was turned, and Finch dimmed the oil-lamp on his desk. Then he fished in his vest pocket, and extracted a key.

'Here you are,' he said, tossing the key to Clem. 'Get the shotgun out. I reckon this should just be a one-shell job.'

Parker went over to a cabinet standing against the far wall. He unlocked it to display an array of firearms from which he selected and loaded a double-barrelled shotgun. Finch, meanwhile, had checked his own sidearms and eased them slightly in their holsters. He gave Farrell, who was still on his feet, a professional survey from head to boots.

'That Colt of yours loaded, Farrell?'

'Of course. Hey, but wait a minute. Me and Mizz Carney are just visitors. If you think we're going to stay and . . .'

77

Finch raised his eyebrows as the clattering of feet on the boardwalk grew ominously louder.

'Seems like you ain't got much choice for the moment.'

As he spoke, someone turned the door handle from the outside, and, when the door failed to open, rattled it impatiently. Then there was a violent rap on the doorframe.

'Hey, Sheriff,' yelled an anonymous voice. 'You in there? Open up, will ya?'

Finch drew one of his pistols and beckoned to Parker.

'Get behind me and level that there shotgun over my shoulder real careful.'

As Parker took up position Finch eased the key in the lock and opened the door slightly, keeping one foot against it to prevent it from swinging wide.

'What in tarnation are you folks doing disturbing the peace at this time of night?' he enquired, addressing himself to the sea of mostly anonymous faces that had gathered outside with only a few flaming torches for illumination.

'Zach's dead, Jade,' called a voice from the front of the crowd. 'And you got the kid that done it. Just send him out and we'll deal with him. It'll be less bother for ya.'

'The hell it will,' said Finch. 'I appreciate your concern, gentlemen, but I'm the law round here and I kind of like to do things the prescribed way. Now you folks just go back to your beds real peaceable. The kid'll get justice.'

'Yeah,' called another voice. 'But when? You know we're real short of judges in this territory. Let's settle it now. We all know the kid did it.'

Finch tightened his lips as a roar of approval followed this last remark and the bolder members of the crowd pressed closer to the door. The sheriff eased his position slightly so that the shotgun wielded by Parker should be clearly visible.

'I already said you ain't got no business here. Now get

your feet off my stoop. Anybody coming any closer is liable to get a blast of shot. I ain't joking. Besides, there's a lady in here and—'

'We ain't jokin' neither,' interrupted another voice. 'And if you got a fancy lady in there, send her out. She won't get hurt.'

At these words, which were clearly audible to the others in the room, Beth Carney rose to her feet with a snort.

'Fancy lady, my foot. Outta my way.'

She pushed Parker and the sheriff aside to show herself at the door. Her appearance elicited a good-humoured cheer which for a moment led Farrell to think that the situation might be defused.

'You boys ought to be ashamed of yourselves acting like a lynch mob. Sheriff just told you he ain't handing over the kid – so just get your hides out of here.'

'We ain't got no quarrel with you, Mizz Carney,' said a man at the front of the crowd. 'Nor with the sheriff. Just come down and someone'll see you back to the Goldrush.'

'I'll go when I'm good and ready,' retorted Beth, turning her back and retreating into the shadows as the sheriff blocked the doorway again.

'That's it boys,' he said decisively. 'You had your marching orders. Now git. If I have to come out again I'll be making arrests.'

With this show of bravado he closed and locked the door to cut off any further discussion. There was a prolonged angry murmur outside, but for the moment nothing happened.

'Jeez,' said Farrell, in tones of admiration. 'You really settled them. That was the coolest . . .'

Finch shook his head.

'They'll be back. They just ain't quite fired up enough yet to take on a shotgun.'

'Oh. What happens then?'

Finch shrugged.

'We hand the kid over. Unless you got any better ideas.'

'Set me up another whiskey.'

'Sure.'

The bartender uncorked the bottle with a covert glance towards his customer perched on a stool at the end of the counter. One of his professional duties was to anticipate that critical moment when one further drink would cause the recipient to crumple blindly to the sawdust, but there was no imminent danger of that. He refilled the glass and slid it across the mahogany.

'Ain't you gonna watch the show?'

Frank McCoy tipped back his hat slightly and took his whiskey in one swallow.

'Seen it before.'

Keeping his back resolutely turned to the stage he doodled a pattern with an absent-minded forefinger in a puddle of beer spilled on the bar top. As he did so, a trim dark-haired figure with a coffee-and-cream complexion tapped him lightly on the wrist. '*Hola*, Franquito.'

McCoy's morose expression lifted as he turned and recognized the girl.

'Hey, Juanita baby. I was just thinking—'

'Buy a girl a drink?' said Juanita, settling herself on the adjacent stool and hitching up her skirt to reveal a very daintily turned ankle.

'Sure.'

'Champagne.'

McCoy nodded to the barman, who had already produced the bottle of cheap house fizz from under the counter.

'I been looking for you all over, Frankie,' said the girl with a slight pout. '*Dónde estuviste?*'

'Back room playing cards.'

80

'*Qué bueno. Y cuanto ganaste?*'

'*Nada de nada.* Guess it wasn't my night.'

'Oh,' said Juanita. 'Naughty boy to lose all your money before I find you.'

'Now why would I do a dang fool thing like that, my little *enchilada*?' grunted McCoy, extending a finger to run it along the top of her bodice. 'I saved enough for you.'

The girl laughed and drew her stool closer so that their knees were touching. McCoy passed her the glass of champagne and ordered up another whiskey for himself. When it was poured he raised his glass to touch hers.

'*Salud.*'

'*Salud,*' said Juanita. '*Y pesos . . . . y tiempo para gastarlos.*'

They bantered inconsequentially for a few minutes and then with a covert glance at the brass railroad clock which hung behind the bar Juanita advanced the more lucrative business of the evening. She leant forward and ran her fingers lightly across the back of McCoy's hand.

'We gonna have some fun tonight, Franquito? I haven't seen you for a whole week. I been real lonely.'

McCoy raised a sceptical eyebrow.

'That so, *querida*?' He slid off the stool and dropped a handful of coins on the bar. 'So what are we waiting for?'

Juanita linked her arm in his and led him across the saloon. They passed through a door at the rear and into a narrow hallway from which a carpeted wooden staircase rose at one end. She led him upstairs to a corridor with rooms opening off on either side. Softly opening one of the doors she motioned McCoy inside.

The room was illuminated by a single oil-lamp set on a table beside a large brass-framed bedstead. A window overlooking Main Street was set into the wall opposite the door, with a marble-topped washstand alongside. McCoy closed the door, deposited his hat on the hatstand and hung his gunbelt beneath it. He advanced to where the girl was standing beside the bed, ran one hand behind the lustrous black curls that covered the nape of her neck and with his other hand tilted her chin up. He stooped slightly so as to make contact with her lips, but as he did so she put up her hand to maintain a slight distance between them.

'*Hombre*, not so fast,' she whispered, 'You know you got to . . .'

McCoy clicked his tongue with impatience.

'I been up here often enough to rate a little credit. Oh well, here . . .' He dug in his pants pocket and produced a ten-dollar bill. 'That enough to satisfy the house rules?'

Juanita's eyes popped as she grasped the note and slid it deftly into a pocket below her waistband.

'*Diablos.* You come into money?' She leant forward and kissed him impulsively.

'Ask no questions,' he muttered, turning her around, '*y no te digo mentiras. . . .*'

He applied practised fingers to the hooks that secured the bodice of her gown, enabling it to slip in a puddle of green satin to the threadbare turkey carpet that covered the floor. Then he worked his way down to the corsetry. When she was settled against the pillows on the bed he sat down beside her ready to pull off his boots. Before he could do so, however, the sound of strident shouting and the trampling of feet began to penetrate through the curtains. McCoy cocked his head towards the window and listened.

'What in tarnation. . . ?'

He stood up, crossed to the window, pulled back the heavy drapes and peered out into the gloom. A crowd of men, some with torches, seemed to be shuffling up Main Street, but it was impossible to see exactly what the cause of the commotion was. He lifted the sash and stuck his head out to get a better view.

'What's going on?' he demanded, shouting down to a

bystander immediately below the window.

'Zach Granger just kicked the bucket and they're goin' to lynch the kid that did it.'

Craning his neck out of the window and looking up the street McCoy was able to see that the crowd was heading for, and congregating outside, the sheriff's office. He pulled his head in and slammed down the sash.

'*Que pasa*, Frankie?' enquired Juanita with an indifferent yawn.

'Lynch mob,' said McCoy, shaking his head in disbelief. 'Ain't seen one of those in these parts for years.'

Juanita patted the bed.

'Come on, Frankie. Get a move on, I'm all ready waiting for you.'

McCoy scratched his head, as if debating something with himself. Then he threw an absent-minded glance towards the recumbent figure on the bed as the sound of the mob outside grew louder.

'What?'

'I said I'm waiting for you. Those men won't come up here, will they?'

McCoy shook his head, but instead of resuming the removal of his boots he crossed to the hatstand, lifted down his gunbelt and began to buckle it on.

'Hey,' said the girl, sitting up with wide-open eyes. 'What are you doing? I thought . . .'

'Sorry, honey. . . .'

McCoy went to the bed, bent down and planted a perfunctory kiss on her forehead. 'First lynching for years and I ain't about to miss it.'

'But—'

'You stay right there and keep the bed warm for me. I don't reckon it'll take long.'

Before she could reply, he had turned, grabbed his hat and opened the door. Juanita spat out a frustrated oath.

'*Hijo de . . .*'

She picked up one of her slippers and shied it towards the retreating figure. But McCoy had already closed the door before the missile clattered harmlessly against the adjacent wall. He walked downstairs and into the crowded saloon. The midnight show was in full swing, and there was so much noise going on that most of the customers seemed unaware of the drama that was unfolding outside. McCoy peered through the tobacco smoke and at last managed to spot a couple of the hands from the Ferguson ranch perched on a wooden settle right against the stage from where they were strategically positioned to enjoy the best of any sights that might be revealed by kicking legs and lifting flounces. McCoy walked across and thumped them on the shoulders to get their attention.

'Outside, boys, you're missing all the real fun.'

'Hey, Frank,' said one of the men. 'We only just sat down. Get a load of this . . .'

McCoy squeezed his shoulder tightly.

'Outside.'

The terseness and urgency of his voice was apparent even through the cacophony of the music and dancing. The two men rose and followed him.

'Thought you might appreciate some real action, boys,' he remarked as they emerged on to the street. 'You can see the show any time, but it's rare enough to be on hand for a real lynching.'

'Better be worth it, Frank. We was all set to see some really pretty ankles back there.' McCoy gave his two companions a withering look.

'Big deal. I was all set to see a sight more than that.'

SEVEN

Farrell stared at the impassive figure of the sheriff.

'Turn the kid over? You serious about that?'

Finch returned his stare. 'Why not? If I don't, they're going to take him anyway. Don't seem no reason for anyone here – including yours truly – to get shot up on account of some cheap trash who ain't got no business in this community in the first place.'

'Yes, but—'

'What's up with you, Farrell?' said Finch in irritation. 'A few minutes ago you was all for not getting yourself mixed up in official business. So what's one no-good kid more or less to you?'

'Nothing,' admitted Farrell reluctantly, as he struggled to make sense of his mixed feelings. 'All the same—'

'All the same, the law's the law,' cut in Beth, completing his thought for him.

Finch turned towards her, his eyebrows raised in amused contempt.

'Why, ain't that just rich.' He chuckled. 'I always figured you for a smart businesswoman, Beth, not a charity worker.'

'Then you ain't figuring far enough, mister,' snapped Beth. 'It's just because I am a smart businesswoman that I ain't keen on seeing you surrender to the mob without a fight. This here's a peaceable town – and a peaceable town's the easiest sort of place to make money in. Let the mob get the idea they can take the law into their own hands and none of us can be sure whose turn it'll be next. What's to stop them busting my saloon if some saddle-sore cahoot figures he don't like my liquor or my prices? You gotta make some sort of stand, Jade, or you've been wasting your time here for the last few years – and we've been paying the wrong man.'

'Trust a woman to want the last word,' muttered Finch in a tone which suggested that he was conceding her point. 'OK, so I come back to my other question. Anyone got any ideas?'

Before anyone could answer, the temporary silence was interrupted by a series of muffled yells accompanied by metallic thumps emanating from somewhere to the rear of the office.

'Son-of-bitch kid,' muttered Finch, jerking his head towards a door in the rear wall. 'Must have realized he's suddenly become the centre of attention.' He walked across, selected a key from a bunch hanging on an adjacent hook and opened the door.

'Hold your goddammed noise back there, will you?' he called into the darkness. Undeterred by the tones of authority the banging continued, followed by the boy's voice.

'Hey, Sheriff. What's goin' on out there?'

'Nothing to concern you. Yet. Now hold your noise.'

During this brief interchange Farrell had taken a moment to assess the details of their surroundings. Like most of the other buildings in the street the sheriff's office was a one-storey clapboard construction. The front and side walls of the room were timber, but the rear wall, which demarcated the cell area into which Finch was now addressing himself, was of brick and plaster. Farrell walked

86

across to the sheriff and peered over his shoulder into the gloom beyond.

'Mind if I take a look?'

Finch shrugged and stood out of his way. Farrell took his place in the doorframe and found himself facing a short corridor lined with iron grilles fronting two small cells on each side. A single oil-lamp hanging on the blank wall at the end provided the only illumination. Farrell advanced a few steps to the second cell on the left, where Ben Ashwood was standing banging a tin mug against the bars. The boy peered at Farrell in the dim light, recognized him and shrank back abruptly from the grille.

'Hey, mister,' he croaked, 'about what happened this morning. I didn't mean—'

'Sure,' snapped Farrell, appraising the prisoner and his accommodation in the uncertain light cast by the oil-lamp. The boy's hair was tousled and a few stray locks were plastered to his forehead with sweat. Bruises on his face, together with a swollen left eye and a cut lip bore testimony to the attention he had earlier received from his custodians. Apart from its occupant the cell itself contained nothing but a wooden bunk partially covered by a rumpled blanket. This was set into the wall facing the grille over which, at about the height of a man's head, was a small barred aperture serving as the only window. It was unglazed and the menacing sounds of the gathering crowd in the street outside were clearly audible.

'What's goin' on out there, mister? What I hear don't sound too friendly.'

'It isn't,' said Farrell tersely. 'Now hush up that noise. We got some thinking to do.' He pulled back, glanced around at the other empty cells and retraced his steps. It was clear that for obvious reasons the jail section of the premises had been more solidly constructed than the part that fronted the main street. Even without the bars the window apertures would have been too small to permit the passage of a man – from either direction. The grilles were firmly set in the masonry, and the door which communicated with the front office was also of iron. Farrell chewed his lip. Since there was clearly no way out at the back they were effectively cornered.

'Kind of a one-way street, ain't it?' he said to Finch, jerking his head back towards the cells. But as he did so, a feature of the corridor which he had previously not noticed in the general gloom caught his eye. In the ceiling a yard or so above his head there was a skylight, presumably inserted to provide illumination during the day. For a moment Farrell's spirits leapt, until he saw that the skylight, too, was protected by an iron grille.

'Pity about them bars,' he said, pointing upwards. 'Maybe we could have gotten out that way.'

'They ain't a fixture,' said Finch. 'Swing right down if you uncatch them.'

Farrell peered upwards again to verify what the sheriff was saying. Instead of being lodged in the brickwork the grille was hinged at one side, being held in place by a padlock at the other. Farrell clutched Finch's arm and propelled him back into the office so that their voices would not carry to the boy in the cell.

'Hey. Maybe we gotta solution. We stall the mob and get the kid out of here over the roof. He can take his chance once he's outside and—'

'Now wait a minute, wait a minute,' interposed Finch. 'It isn't that easy. The kid may not be lynch-mob fodder but he's still a legitimate prisoner wanted for manslaughter. If I set him scot free I'll be the next target for the rope.'

'Yes, but . . .'

Before Farrell could frame his objection there was a sudden loud roar from the crowd outside, followed by the smashing of glass as a brick crashed through the blinds and fetched up with a crack against the sheriff's desk.

'Lands sakes,' muttered Beth, twitching her skirt away from the splinters, 'You two gonna stand there arguing all night? Things is about to get serious.'

As if to confirm her words a voice shouted through the newly created aperture in the windowframe.

'You can hear us real good, now, sheriff. Quit stalling and send the kid out.'

With an oath Finch grabbed the shotgun from Parker, knelt under the shattered window and unleashed a couple of shells, firing high so as to shoot over the crowd's heads. The sound of the shots was followed by a sudden silence, and then the crashing of boots as those on the boardwalk outside scattered for cover.

'Come on man,' urged Farrell. 'We're running out of time. You gotta a key to that padlock?'

'Sure,' grunted Finch as he reloaded, 'but I just told you that—'

'Aw shucks,' interrupted Farrell, who had been doing his own thinking while Finch was wielding the shotgun. 'I'll stick with the kid myself. Hide him out till things quieten down and then hand him back to you.'

'Yeah?' Finch's tone was deeply sceptical. 'Hide him out where exactly? You got a bolt-hole all lined up ready?'

'No,' admitted Farrell. 'But—'

'But I have.' Beth's voice cut decisively through the interchange. 'Cover him up and slip him into my room at the saloon. You oughta be able to work your way round to the back door and get him up the stairs. It's the last place anyone would think of looking for him.'

Farrell stared at her. A few minutes ago he had been frantic to disengage himself from the entire situation; now despite his own better judgement he found himself being swept along by the excitement of the moment. He turned to Finch.

'It might just work if we—'

'Sure it'll work,' cut in Beth, pulling off her shawl and mantilla and thrusting them into Farrell's hands. 'Here's my contribution. Dress the kid up in these. It's too dark out there for anyone to notice the size of his boots.'

There was no time to be lost. The jeers and catcalls from outside were becoming ever more threatening, and it would clearly only be a matter of moments before the bolder spirits in the mob worked up enough courage to force their way in.

'Come on, Sheriff. Give me the key to that lock, will you?'

'Here,' said Finch, tossing him the bunch from which he had opened the rear door. 'It's one of the small ones.'

Farrell hefted the keys and flicked through them with mounting desperation as another brick crashed through the window. There were several small keys that might have fitted a padlock.

'Yeah, but which one, for Pete's sake. They all look alike.'

'Anyone's guess,' said Finch, loosing off another couple of shells through the window. 'Can't remember when we last had it open.'

'Oh, Jesus,' muttered Farrell. He grabbed a chair, thrust it under the skylight, mounted it and began to apply the most likely keys in quick succession to the rusty padlock. The dimness of the glow from the oil-lamp made the insertion of each key a trial of patience in itself. At last, after what seemed an eternity but was probably less than a couple of minutes, his fumbling efforts bore fruits as he found a key that turned stiffly in the lock, springing the padlock open. Flicking it aside, Farrell applied his weight to the bars. At first nothing happened, and then with a shower of rust and grime the grille swung down on its hinges. Farrell thrust up his hand to examine the window, finding to his annoyance that it was a fixture. With a muffled curse he climbed down from the chair and returned to the office.

'Gonna have to break another of your windows,' he yelled across at Finch.

'Big deal,' muttered Finch, as the timber frame of the office door began to shudder from the weight of the bodies being thrust against it from outside. Farrell grabbed Beth's shawl from the desk where he had discarded it, wrapped it around his pistol and returned to the skylight. Hoping that the shawl would muffle any sound which would alert those outside to what was going on, he applied the pistol butt to the window, and with a few vigorous whacks smashed the glass out of the frame. Now for the kid. Farrell ran to the cell and pulled impotently at the bars. The cell door was locked, of course, and the keys were on the desk where he had thrown them on picking up the shawl. With an even louder curse Farrell dashed back to the office to find Parker and Finch dragging the desk against the threatened front door. The bunch of keys was nowhere in sight.

'The keys, the goddammed keys,' shouted Farrell as a shot exploded from just outside the door and the timber around the door lock splintered under the impact of a bullet. 'Over there,' pointed Beth, indicating where the keys had fallen into a corner as the desk was shifted. Farrell stooped to retrieve them, noting with dismay that there were several which might have opened a cell.

'Last of the big ones,' said Finch tersely.

Farrell separated the key, returned to the corridor and unlocked Ashwood's cell. The boy, who had been sitting on the bunk, stood up as Farrell swung back the door.

'Will you for chrissake tell me what's goin' on, mister,' he began, as Farrell unfurled Beth's shawl and wrapped it around his shoulders.

'Shut up and listen good,' snarled Farrell, thrusting him back against the cell wall with enough violence to knock the breath out of his body. 'The old boy you knocked down this morning just died and the townsfolk want your neck for it.'

'But I—'

'Shut up, will you. 'Stead of turning you over to the wolves we're trying to get you out of here. So don't argue – just do exactly as you're told or you're dead meat.'

He grabbed the boy by the shoulder and hustled him out into the corridor. Farrell adjusted the chair under the shattered fanlight and prepared to climb up.

'Here,' said Finch, who had temporarily abandoned his position at the office door. 'Use these in case sonny here gets any bright ideas about taking off permanently.' He thrust a pair of handcuffs into Farrell's fist.

'Right.'

But Farrell hesitated. They had to get on to the roof first, and the kid would need both hands for that. He tucked the cuffs into his belt, mounted the chair, and levered himself upward through the aperture through which the baying of the mob was now sounding uncomfortably close. As Farrell exposed his head into the darkness, he felt the momentary sensation of a circus performer entering a cage of particularly dangerous and unpredictable lions.

Frank McCoy was elbowing his way through the throng which was collecting along Main Street when a thought struck him. He put a restraining hand on his companion's shoulder.

'Just a minute. You got a rope on your saddle?'

'A rope? Sure. But what do you need. . . .'

'We're headed for a lynching, right? Can't have a lynch-

92

ing without a rope.'

'Oh.'

They retraced their steps to where the horses were teth-ered to the hitching rail outside the saloon. McCoy detached a coil of rope from one of the saddles, looped it round his shoulder, and led the way up the street. There was a sizeable press of people around the sheriff's office and in the flickering of the lights from the various flaming torches that some of the crowd were carrying McCoy could make out a couple of bolder spirits applying their shoulders to the sagging door.

'What's going on, boys?' he shouted to a couple of men standing at the back of the mob. The noise was now so great that he could scarcely hear the reply.

'They want the kid that did for Zach this morning, but Finch ain't in any hurry to hand him over.'

'Shame.'

McCoy worked his way with difficulty to the front of the mob just as the door finally gave way. There was a whoop of triumph from the assembled company as the men who had been applying their weight almost fell into the inte-rior. When it became obvious that the way inside was open there was a general surge forward which carried McCoy through the doorway. The lights had been dowsed, and until a few torches had been handed through it was diffi-cult to make anything out. There was a momentary silence.

'Hey, there ain't nobody here.'

The office was indeed empty, but the onward rush of the intruders was scarcely checked.

'Through the back,' somebody yelled, rushing to the door which led to the cells. He rattled the handle impo-tently.

'Hey, Sheriff. Open this goddammed door, will you? Or we'll bust the place wide open.'

He rattled the handle again. There was a pause, and then Finch's voice could be heard from the other side of the door.

'OK boys. Ease up, will you? I'm opening the door. But remember I got a shotgun and a rifle pointing straight ahead.'

The crowd eased back slightly as they heard the sound of a key turning in the lock. The door swung open to reveal the figure of Finch standing with a shotgun levelled straight at the heads of the nearest men. Behind him loomed the figure of Parker with a rifle similarly aimed.

'Hand the kid over, Jade, and quit pussyfooting. We ain't going till we get him.'

'I heard you. Now just ease back will you. Me and Clem wouldn't want to get in your way.'

Finch and his assistant stepped forward and backed along the rear wall of the office, firearms still raised.

'OK, boys,' urged one of the men by the door. 'Let's get the kid.'

They dashed into the corridor beyond and wrenched open the door of one of the cells where a figure was sitting on the bunk.

'What the—'

'Evening boys,' said Beth Carney, rising from her perch and making her way into the passage. There was a sudden scrabble as the searchers checked the other cells and realized that their quarry had escaped.

' 'Fraid you've been wasting your time, gentlemen,' said Finch. 'The kid busted out through the roof.'

There was a howl of rage from the intruders.

'You mean you let him bust out, you tricky son of a bitch.'

'Whatever.'

Finch's voice was calm but behind the sights of the shotgun his eyes were alert for any sign that the mob was likely to take him as a substitute victim. However, the tension was resolved as one of the men emerged from the passage and pushed his way towards the street.

'Come on, boys. The kid can't be far away. Let's go get him.'

The crowd suddenly withdrew and scattered, leaving Beth to pick her way across the shattered glass and other debris from the rampage as Finch and Parker lowered their weapons.

'Well,' she said to the remaining laggards. 'I guess that's quite enough excitement for tonight. If you'll excuse me I'll go home.'

A figure detached itself from the shadows by the door.

'If you'll allow me, ma'am, I'll see you across the street.'

'What?' Beth narrowed her eyes in an effort to make out who was addressing her. 'Oh, it's you, Frank McCoy.' She studied his proffered arm for a moment and then stalked past on to the porch. 'Guess I can find my own way home, thank you.'

As McCoy stared at her retreating back his companion tapped him on the shoulder.

'Hey, Frank. Aren't you joining the hunt. They ain't going to let the kid get away.'

'What? No. Don't feel like joining in a wild-goose chase. Kid could be anywhere in the dark. Besides, I got some unfinished business.'

He strode off in Beth's wake towards the saloon.

After taking a moment to adjust his eyes to the dark Farrell turned his head cautiously to left and right. Breathing a sigh of relief he saw that as yet the flat roof had attracted no attention from the besiegers. In any case the clapboard frontage of the office had been continued upward beyond roof-level for some three feet as a sort of balustrade, so as long as they kept their heads down they would be effectively screened from the street. He pulled himself through and then flattened himself face down so as to speak through the skylight.

'Up here, kid – and keep flat as soon as you're through.'

Ashwood's face quickly appeared through the hole and Farrell extended a hand to his collar, almost dragging him upwards by the scruff of his neck. When the kid was lying flat on the roof beside him Farrell drew his Colt and prodded him sharply in the side with the barrel.

'Listen good, kiddo. I can't put the cuffs on because you may need your hands to get down from here. But you make one false move and I'll plug you for real. You're still in custody, remember.'

Farrell gave the boy another admonitory jab with the pistol and motioned him to lie still for a moment. Then he edged himself to the side of the roof furthest from the street to reconnoitre a means of escape. The noise from the mob seemed to be all around them, but peering down over the rear wall Farrell was relieved to find that nobody had moved around the back of the premises. An unlit, narrow alley ran parallel with the main street offering an immediate means of escape provided that they were not intercepted. There was no time to lose. From somewhere down below Farrell heard another smash of splintering glass accompanied by a triumphant swelling of the noise from the mob. He beckoned to Ashwood.

'Over here, and keep your head down.'

As the kid slithered across, Farrell swung his legs down into the darkness and lowered himself over the edge, dangling for a few moments by his fingertips. The height of the roof was about twelve feet and the drop to the ground was, of course, lessened by the length of Farrell's body. He braced himself, relaxed his knees and released his grip on the roof. He landed in soft earth, but one of his boots slid off the edge of a protruding rock, giving his ankle an unwelcome wrench. Farrell cursed, righted himself and peered up towards where Ashwood's pale face was visible on the roof line.

'All clear. Get yourself down here pronto.'

Ashwood swung himself over, dropped, and landed beside Farrell in the alley. Farrell hauled him to his feet and adjusted his drapery.

'OK. Let's get the hell outta here. Take my arm.'

Ashwood looked at him blankly.

'What?'

'Take my arm, for Pete's sake. We got to look like some couple taking the evening air. Less chance of being noticed that way.'

Ashwood obediently took Farrell's left arm and they stumbled through the darkness towards the end of the alley. Even as they did so Farrell heard a further burst of frustrated yelling from inside the jail, followed by a change in volume and direction, as though the mob were spilling back into the street.

'Must have discovered that we've bust out,' muttered Farrell. 'They'll be all over the place now. Remember I've still got my right arm free,' he said, bundling Ashwood into another side alley. 'And I meant what I said about shooting you if you try running off.'

'I heard you, mister.'

It was obvious from the swelling of noise that a hue and cry was now being raised all through town. Farrell took no chances, being uncomfortably aware that, in the present state of excitement, if they were detected it might not only be Ashwood's neck that was at risk. With pounding heart he led the kid methodically by back alleys, not regaining Main Street until they were at least two hundred yards down from the scene of action. Then they promenaded demurely across the street to a side lane and approached the saloon from behind quite unnoticed.

This was unfamiliar territory and Farrell surveyed the rear of the building with some uncertainty. However, a few dim lights from the windows provided enough illumination for him to make out the back door. He nudged the kid towards it, fearful that any moment someone might open the door and spot them. But they reached it without incident, and having checked that nobody was approaching from either direction, Farrell gingerly tried the handle. The door creaked open and Farrell peered inside.

A passageway lit by a single suspended oil-lamp appeared to run the length of the building. There were doors in the opposite wall presumably leading through to the public parts of the premises. The usual sounds of merriment were clearly audible. If anyone came into the passage now, Farrell and his charge would be instantly spotted. To the left a narrow wooden staircase, almost as steep as a ladder, led to the upper floor. Farrell bundled the boy inside and prodded him up the stairs which terminated in another door. Farrell edged it open with extreme caution. Another hallway stretched out in both directions, but this was much more spacious and well lit, with doors on either side. A generous expanse of red turkey-carpet spread to the end where a wide staircase led down to the saloon – allowing the noise from below to pound up loud and clear.

Farrell pulled Ashwood through, but it was only when they had advanced a few steps that Farrell realized that he hadn't the faintest idea how to locate Beth's bedroom. He knew from previous visits that several of the rooms were used by the bar hostesses for their temporary clients, but Beth had failed to indicate which was her own particular sanctum, and of course, in the urgency of the moment back in the sheriff's office, he had failed to ask the obvious question.

'Which way, mister?' whispered Ashwood, tugging at his arm.

Farrell chewed his lip in irritation.

'How the hell . . .'

Farrell stopped himself in mid-response. This was no time to display uncertainty. He grabbed the kid by the shoulder and bundled him along to the first door on the left. With a silent prayer that the room wouldn't be in occupation Farrell tried the handle. The door was locked. As Farrell released his grip with a curse he heard the unmistakable sounds of heavy boots coming up the main staircase. If they didn't get out of sight immediately they would be cornered. There was no time to retrace their steps, so Farrell lunged across the hall and tried the door opposite. To his relief, it opened. He pushed the kid inside and closed the door. The room was empty, but bore recent traces of occupation. A lamp was burning, and the bedclothes were rumpled. No matter: the mission was accomplished and the kid would be reasonably safe. What happened thereafter would be Finch's problem. Farrell extracted the handcuffs from his belt and snatched off the mantilla and shawl with which Ashwood had been disguised. He spun the boy around, pulled one hand behind his back and sprang the cuff firmly shut over his wrist.

'Hey,' protested Ashwood. 'What ya doing? I haven't given no trouble. You can keep me covered with your pistol.'

'The hell I can,' said Farrell. 'I've done enough nurse-maiding for tonight, mister. I'm out of here, and you can wait till the sheriff gets round to you. Meantime, if you're shackled to that there bed you won't be going anywhere.' He pushed the boy over the bed, with the intention of fixing the other half of the manacles to the brass frame, but before he could snap it shut the footsteps which he had heard coming up the stairs approached the bedroom door. As Farrell froze in confusion, the door was flung open. There was silence for a moment, and then a familiar voice spoke.

'Well, son-of-a-gun,' chuckled Frank McCoy. 'Looks like I'm intruding on something real personal.' He advanced into the room, kicked the door shut behind him and surveyed the tableau of Farrell, boy, handcuffs, bed and discarded drapery with a sardonic leer.

'I guess I owe you an apology, Farrell. Looks like I figured you and Miss Hetty all wrong. You should have told me you was a—'

'Goddammit, McCoy,' grunted Farrell, straightening up and turning to face the other man. 'You got a reason for barging in here?'

'Just a matter of unfinished personal business,' chuckled McCoy, gesturing towards the rumpled bed. 'Looks like the young lady got tired of waiting. But maybe you're right. Ain't no call for me to be interrupting your own personal business – 'less you'd like an audience, that is. I mean . . . I've often wondered what—'

'Keep your goddam thoughts to yourself,' snarled Farrell, feeling his face go crimson with embarrassment and exasperation at the expression of prurient superiority plastered all over McCoy's features. Suddenly all the psychological advantage he had gained over the other man at the card-table seemed in danger of catastrophic reversal. 'This ain't personal business, it's official.'

Almost as soon as the words had left his mouth Farrell regretted them. It was maddening that McCoy was attributing an obscene interpretation to the scenario, but he was only doing so because he had no idea who Ashwood was. Now, hearing the word 'official', his demeanour changed and he stepped forward to scrutinize the lad more closely.

'Official? What do you mean?'

McCoy glanced down at the discarded clothing, registered the bruises on Ashwood's sallow face and had no difficulty this time in making the right deduction.

'Why, I do believe you've got the kid they've all been shouting for outside Finch's office.'

'Like I said, McCoy, it's official business. Now get the hell out of here, and keep your mouth shut about what you've seen. The kid's the property of the sheriff.'

'The heck he is. Seems like the townsfolk are taking a different view.'

McCoy pointed towards the half-open window through which the frustrated baying of a crowd cheated of its quarry could clearly be heard. Then he menacingly hefted the length of rope which was still coiled around his shoulder.

'Kind of a pity to disappoint them.'

'Hey,' yelled Farrell, stepping forward to interpose himself between McCoy and his intended victim, 'you can't . . .'

But before he could complete the sentence Ashwood had taken matters into his own hands. With McCoy blocking the way to the door the boy bolted for his only other means of escape and thrust himself head first through the window.

'Crazy son-of-a-gun,' yelled Farrell, wheeling round in frustration. The window was the best part of twenty feet above the street, and there was no balcony to break any fall. But McCoy, who had been facing the kid, was even quicker in his reaction. Brushing Farrell aside he darted to the window in time to slam down the sash on the heel of one of Ashwood's retreating boots. With a grunt of satisfaction at seeing the would-be fugitive pinned tight, he smashed one of the window panes with his elbow and leaned out to survey his handiwork. Ashwood, suspended

101

by one leg, was sprawled head down, his fingers scrabbling desperately against the clapboard wall of the saloon in a frantic attempt to gain some purchase to lever himself upright. The smashing of the glass had already attracted attention so that McCoy's triumphant yell was almost superfluous.

'Hey, boys,' he called down into the darkness, 'this what you're looking for?'

Within seconds a crowd of men, some of them still bearing torches, rushed over to where Ashwood was hanging impotently. From inside the bedroom Farrell could hear a collective whoop of joy as they identified their prey. He rushed over and grabbed McCoy by the shoulder.

'We gotta get him back in here. They'll tear him to pieces.'

'Sure they will,' said McCoy. 'So what?'

Farrell stared at him in disbelief.

'So what? You wanna be party to a lynching for chris'sake?'

McCoy shrugged as he continued to peer down at the struggling figure pinned helplessly above the gathering mob. When he spoke his voice was as calm as if he were looking out on an Independence Day parade.

'Kind of a shame to spoil their fun.'

'Fun?'

Farrell found himself almost struck dumb with anger against the callousness of McCoy's demeanour, but he made one last effort to take control of the situation. Grabbing a precarious hold of the wriggling foot that was still protruding into the room he urged McCoy into a minimum gesture of assistance.

'Lift the sash, man, while I try to haul him back.'

As McCoy remained motionless, Farrell repeated his plea in tones of desperation.

'Come on, Frank. Do it, will you?'

McCoy scowled with contempt and then thrust the sash abruptly upwards. Farrell was already leaning back, bracing his feet against the wainscot, to take the strain of Ashwood's weight. But as the pressure on his ankle suddenly lifted Ashwood seemed to wriggle his foot half out of the encasing boot. Gravity did the rest. Before he could adjust his grasp Farrell found himself clutching an empty boot as the boy fell head first with a despairing scream to hit the street. There was a jeer of triumph from his would-be tormentors, followed by a moment of total silence. With a puzzled frown Farrell shoved the sash fully open and leant out. A couple of men with torches were kneeling by the prostrate figure. After a pause one of them stood up and shook his head in annoyance.

'Looks like the show's over, boys. Goddammed kid's gone and bust his neck.'

EIGHT

The shaving-mirror was cracked and discoloured but it revealed enough of Farrell's face to produce a momentary grimace of self-disgust. He applied the razor to the last patch of soap and squinted at the finished result. Scarcely the face of a hero, he thought, as he rubbed it with a scrap of rough towelling. He wiped the razor and flicked it shut. Then he tucked it in his shirt pocket and walked outside. It was only the breakfast hour but the sun was already bright and the sudden contrast with the gloom of the bunkhouse momentarily stung his eyes. He walked across to the cookhouse and poked his head in the door. Inside, Lee was tossing strips of bacon on to a griddle.

'Hi, Mr Matt.'

'Uh huh.' Farrell's response was gruff. He reached into his pocket and slid the razor across.

'Put an edge on this sometime, will you. Can't seem to get it properly honed nohow.'

'Sure.'

Lee stared at him.

'You having breakfast? Horn went ten minutes ago.'

'Yeah, I heard it.'

'Kind of a late night, huh?'

'Kind of.'

Lee's face was a study in polite curiosity, but somehow

104

Farrell felt disinclined to provide any amplification of what the cook had presumably already picked up from the hands who had been in town the night before. It had indeed been a late night and he only had the scantiest recollection of the ride back to the ranch in the early hours of the morning. From the moment young Ashwood had fallen to the ground Farrell's brain had been burning with a sense of personal failure, and even when he had at last crashed into his bunk sleep had eluded him. His mission seemed to have gone from success to failure in a matter of seconds and he found himself constantly rehashing the sequence of events to work out whether he could have taken any action which would have averted the final catastrophe. It was now Sunday morning and he found himself viewing the prospect of the more relaxed routines of the Sabbath with actual distaste. A hard day's grind in the saddle would really have been a welcome distraction. He sighed.

'Talk to you later, Lee.'

'Sure thing.'

Farrell turned and walked round to where the other hands were already seated at a trestle-table having breakfast. Usually conversation at the morning hour was confined to grunts and yawns, but today it was animated – at least until Farrell appeared. As one of the younger men edged along the bench to allow Farrell room to sit down a constrained silence fell on the company. At last Jim Lester broke the spell.

'Pass you something, Matt?'

'Just coffee.'

The pot was passed along. Farrell filled his mug and took a swig. It was only lukewarm – the penalty for arriving late. He could have sent the pot back to Lee for a refill, but what the hell. Blunt razor, cold coffee . . . maybe this was a day for self-punishment. He rested his elbows on the table and contemplated the muddy liquid in his mug. As the silence persisted he looked up and stared aggressively around.

'Something wrong?'

'Nope,' said Lester in emollient tones. 'Boys was just filling me in on what happened in town last night. Seems I missed a real show. Just my luck.'

'Sure,' conceded Farrell, 'if that's how you wanna look at it. Seeing a kid break his neck ain't my kind of entertainment.'

'Hey,' protested Lester, 'I never suggested—'

'Take it easy, Matt,' intervened Wilson. 'Jim was only catching up on the news. Ain't every week that Pinedale Fork goes crazy. Seems we all got a little overexcited. We didn't know you was in that office with the sheriff. You could have all got yourselves burnt up the way feelings were running. It was you getting the kid out that cooled things down. Maybe it worked out for the best.'

'Not for the kid,' said Farrell.

Wilson looked at him in some perplexity.

'Sure. But he weren't . . . I mean . . . never figured you for a . . .'

'Tender heart?' chuckled McCoy from the end of the table.

'Well . . . somethin' like that,' muttered Wilson, eyeing Farrell's thunderous expression nervously. 'Anyway, the kid weren't nothing special . . .'

'Yeah?' guffawed McCoy, leaning back from the table. 'Who to? Well, tender ain't the word. You should have seen the pair of them when I bust in to Juanita's room. Why, I reckon if I hadn't showed up Farrell here would have been all set to—'

'Cut it out, McCoy,' said Farrell clenching his fist around his tin mug as the company hooted in ribald laughter.

106

'Just filling the boys in, Farrell – if you'll pardon the expression. Guess they never knew they was messing with a *mamanachos.*'

As the derisive laughter erupted again, Farrell's temper exploded. He had had enough experience as a ranch hand to know all about the routine ribbing and rough-housing that took place around the meal-table and in the bunkhouse. It was generally without malice and you just had to learn to take it, grin, and give as good as you got. But he understood, even if the other men didn't, that McCoy's gibe went far beyond the boundaries of normal good-natured chaff. It was surely aimed as a stinging insult to his manhood and Farrell read it as exactly that. Flinging the dregs of his coffee into McCoy's face he sprang up, grabbed him by the collar and dragged him backwards from his seat.

'I said shut up, goddammit,' said Farrell, hurling the startled foreman to the ground. McCoy hit the ground with a grunt, took a moment to brush the splashes of coffee from his face, and scrambled to his feet. In a matter of seconds his expression passed from surprise to anger and eventually to a sort of sinister satisfaction. When he spoke his voice was almost glacial.

'OK, Farrell. So you want to make a fight of it? Get your ass over to the corral, mister. I'm gonna teach you a lesson you'll never forget.'

Farrell glanced round at the immobile faces of his colleagues as if looking for some outward sign of support. But as the other men remained silent he shrugged, turned his back, and strode off to the corrals with McCoy stalking behind him. The occasional fistfight was a fact of life in a situation where a lot of young men were cooped up together, and a corral was the usual place where scores would be settled. Farrell selected an empty pen, vaulted over the fencing, stripped off his shirt and hung it on the

107

nearest post. McCoy did likewise as the other hands came scrambling up to allocate themselves ringside positions atop the palings so as to miss none of the action.

As McCoy followed his example and stripped to the waist Farrell made a rapid calculation of his chances. Looking at McCoy's well-honed torso, which appeared to be all muscle and no fat, Farrell saw no particular grounds for optimism that the foreman would be an easy pushover. On the other hand he was Farrell's senior by at least four or five years which surely meant that he wouldn't have the agility of the younger man. Or would he? There was only one way to find out.

So, allowing McCoy no time to collect himself, Farrell hurled himself into the fray, rushing straight at him, feinting a jab with his left hand, ducking under McCoy's hastily improvised counter-punch and delivering a right-hander to the point of his jaw with all the strength he could muster. McCoy's head jerked back under the force of the impact, and before he could recover Farrell followed through with a crashing left-hander into his ribs. The suddenness of the assault combined with the force of the two punches pitched McCoy off balance. As he sprawled on his back in the dust Farrell went for the kill.

There were no rules for this sort of contest, of course, and nothing was barred. He drew back his foot and landed his boot with a flying kick into McCoy's midriff. McCoy grunted and writhed in a sort of half-roll away from Farrell's legs. But as Farrell closed up to complete the operation McCoy suddenly reversed the direction of his roll, throwing his body against Farrell's boots. Unable to check the impetus of his attended attack Farrell stumbled face forward over McCoy's body and hit the ground. Even as he did so McCoy was on his feet, and as Farrell levered himself half-upright McCoy was on him, driving his knee into Farrell's unprotected face and sending him sprawling.

Farrell was vaguely aware of excited cheering and encouragement from the onlookers, but there was no time to worry about who they were shouting for, because as he lay looking up at the sky McCoy hurled himself on top of him, pinning him to the ground and hammering his fists into his chest with almost manic fury. Unable to retaliate, Farrell could only clutch desperately at McCoy's shoulders in a vain attempt to restrain the severity of the bombardment, while trying to prise his body from under his opponent's weight. As the blows rained down Farrell at last managed to wriggle free and thrust McCoy away from him. Taking advantage of this temporary release he rolled aside and managed to regain his feet. McCoy did likewise, and with scarcely a pause for breath they grappled again, trading punches and kicks in a whirlwind of dust.

If Farrell had had time to notice anything but the ferocious determination of his opponent he would have become aware that the ringside hooting and hollering had totally subsided, and that apart from the dogged grunts and oaths of the two pugilists the corral was totally silent. As the fight continued it had become apparent to the onlookers that this was no ordinary random scrap between two cowboys who would trade desultory blows for five or ten minutes until one of them fell over or until some diplomatic third party negotiated an honourable truce which would enable them to shake hands and go off to the nearest saloon together. A real struggle for survival was taking place right there in front of them and no one was more conscious of this than Farrell. What was worse, although at this stage the spectators were probably not aware of it, was a creeping certainty that he was losing.

Hetty Ferguson tilted her head to admire the effect of the new bonnet, made an inessential cosmetic adjustment, and tied the ribbons.

'That what cost me five dollars?'

Hetty transferred her gaze to the face which had loomed behind her in the mirror. She smiled innocently.

'Worth every cent, Pa.' She turned round and patted her bodice. 'Ain't it a perfect match for this blue dress? You ought to be proud to have such a well-turned-out daughter.'

Ferguson grunted, but the twinkle in his eye signalled no dissent from this proposition.

'That's as maybe. A son would have been cheaper. And I don't remember your ma demanding a new outfit every week. If she had, we'd never have made a go of this place. I'd have been bankrupt before we branded the first steer.'

'Well, times change, Pa. And it isn't every week. I keep switching things around to confuse you.'

'Even so,' muttered Ferguson. 'Don't seem right doing all that titivating just for church. What's wrong with plain black?'

'Nothing – as long as it's for funerals. Anyway, black doesn't suit me. Like Ma I prefer to leave it to you men.'

Hetty stepped back, surveyed her father and frowned slightly.

'Speaking of which, why haven't you got your Sunday best on? Don't want to be late.'

'Because I ain't coming.'

'But. . . ?'

Ferguson shook his head.

'But nothing. My arthritis is giving me hell and I don't fancy a long jolt in that confounded surrey, and the same jolt back – with an hour in a hard pew sandwiched in between. You can make my apologies to Reverend Fletcher and I'll give you extra for the collection as conscience money. Just make sure everybody sees you put it in. All right?'

'If you say so. Seems a pity you'll miss out on the fun, though.'

'Fun? Since when was churchgoing fun? You tog yourself up like you were going to some Mardi Gras parade and . . .' Ferguson broke off and clutched his daughter's hand as a worrying thought struck him. 'You ain't got a follower in town? Some fancy. . . ?'

Hetty wriggled her hand free and laughed.

'Oh Pa, you're priceless. Maybe *fun* was the wrong word. Damage might be better.'

'Damage?'

'Sure. Seems like tempers got a little high in town last night and the good citizens bust up the sheriff's office. Almost a lynching, I hear.'

'What?' Ferguson's eyebrows shot up in disbelief. 'And exactly who did you hear it from? Surely you ain't been hobnobbing with the hands already this morning when I've told you a dozen times—'

'No, I haven't. Rosa told me.'

'Rosa? Don't tell me you let the maid go sashaying into town on a Saturday night.'

'I didn't. She got it from Lee, who got it from the boys. So there.'

Ferguson scratched his head.

'Lynching? Well, I'll be doggoned . . .'

'I said "almost", Pa. And Matt Farrell was involved somehow.'

'Farrell?'

'So Rosa says. Pity you'll be missing out on all the up-to-date news. But never mind. I can drive myself in and—'

'Whoa there, young lady,' interrupted Ferguson, holding up his hand. 'You're not driving in alone. You know the rules. I'll get one of the hands to sit with you.'

Hetty clicked her tongue with impatience.

'Oh, Pa. I can manage the surrey by myself. It isn't

111

exactly a stagecoach. For heaven's sake don't fuss.'

'I'm not fussing,' said Ferguson. He threw open the front door and stepped on to the front porch. 'I'm just telling you what's going to happen whether you like it or not. And if you . . .'

Ferguson broke off with a frown of irritation as he scanned the pathway in front of the house. The Sunday morning carriage-ride to church was part of the fixed routines of the ranch, and it was the duty of one of the hands in rotation to harness up and prepare the surrey for its weekly outing and have it outside the house at ten o'clock sharp. But this morning it was nowhere in sight.

'What in tarnation . . .' muttered Ferguson, turning round and squinting into the hallway to check the time by the grandfather clock. 'Young lady, looks like you'll be walking into town for all anyone around here cares.'

He scanned across to the distant outbuildings, but nobody was in sight. And apart from the occasional bellowing from the cattle out on the far pasture there was no sound of activity. Ferguson set his jaw in annoyance, stumped inside and gave a violent shake to the handbell that stood on one of the side tables. When the maid came scuttling out from the rear of the premises he permitted himself a grunt of satisfaction.

'At least someone's alive round here.'

Farrell was pinned against one of the corner posts of the corral and McCoy's fists were drumming like sledgehammers into his ribs. He lifted his knee and managed to jerk it into McCoy's stomach with enough force to throw the other man on to his back foot. Taking advantage of the slight space that had opened between them Farrell slipped out of the corner and swiped blindly at McCoy's face. His fist slid off the sweat that glistened on McCoy's discoloured cheekbone and glanced harmlessly across the

112

'You just got lucky, Farrell, but I ain't finished with you.'

He turned on his heel, grabbed his shirt, left the corral and without looking round headed straight for the nearest water trough. There he paused to duck his head a couple of times and then dried off some of the surplus water with his shirt. Having straightened up he strode off towards the house, pulling on his shirt *en route*. Ferguson was standing on the porch with a face like thunder.

'Any idea what the time is?' asked Ferguson as McCoy reached the steps.

McCoy looked momentarily bewildered as if he thought that Ferguson had called him over just to check the time.

'Why no, boss. I was just attending to—'

'It's past ten o'clock,' cut in Ferguson. 'And whatever you was attending to, doesn't seem it had anything to do with getting my daughter to church.'

McCoy glanced up at Miss Hetty in her Sunday finery and back at the space where the trap should have been ready waiting. He brushed some wet strands of hair away from his eyes and winced.

'Sorry, boss. I clean forgot you'd be—'

'Standing here high and dry while you attend to personal business. First time I ever knew Sunday morning take you by surprise – specially as they come round regular as clockwork.'

'I know, sir. I was . . .'

'You was what?' enquired Ferguson, descending a couple of steps so as to get a better view of his foreman's face. 'Goddammed fighting by the look of you. Someone roughed up your face real good. Who was it?'

McCoy hung his head, and paused before replying.

'I was teaching one of the hands some manners, boss. But it doesn't matter. It's over now. I'll get someone to bring the trap round.'

He turned to go, but Ferguson stopped him.

'Pardon me, mister, you won't get anyone to do it. You can see to it yourself.'

'Yes, sir.'

'And smarten yourself up, as you'll be sitting up there with my daughter.'

McCoy frowned. 'You mean. . . . ?'

'I mean you'll be going with her. I'm not feeling up to it myself, so dust your boots off.'

'But, boss, I can easily—'

'Find another man to do it. Yeah, I'm sure. But I'm saying you can do it yourself as you seem to have time on your hands.'

McCoy turned away with a scowl on his face and made off towards the outbuildings. On his way to the shed where the trap and other vehicles were stored he passed the corral where Farrell, surrounded by several of the other men, was buttoning on his shirt. Farrell clenched his fists as if expecting McCoy to renew the fray, but the foreman simply paused long enough to give him a baleful glare before disappearing round the corner.

'Might at least have offered to shake hands with you,' muttered Charlie Wilson, as he brushed some of the accumulated dust off Farrell's pants. 'You fought him fair and square.'

'Yeah,' agreed Jim Lester. 'Kind of a pity it finished like that. Another coupla minutes, Matt, and you would have whipped him real good.'

Farrell, who had been standing in something of a daze ever since McCoy abandoned the corral, shook his head in bewilderment at what he was hearing.

'Well, of course, I . . .'

'Sure,' put in one of the men. 'First time I ever see anyone stand up to Frank for longer than it takes my old granny to skin a rabbit. Jesus, you really caught him some good ones.'

'Yes, but . . .'

Farrell was about to make a modest confession of his own inadequacy when he was interrupted by another friendly fist clapping him enthusiastically on the shoulder.

'Well done, *compadre*. You licked the foreman. Ain't never seen anything like it.' Farrell winced under the friendly accolade, which had caught him on a particularly sore spot, but decided to abandon his attempt at self-deprecation. Amidst the chorus of congratulation he was almost able to persuade himself that he had, indeed, been winning. He could have pointed out that a bit of similar vocal encouragement when he was actually undergoing his ordeal would have been even more helpful, but this was no time to be churlish. He let himself be escorted over to the trough to have his head ducked long and hard. And then he found Lee dragging him over to the cookhouse.

'I got some fresh coffee brewing for you, Mr Matt,' said the cook, pointing at the range. 'And this . . .' He reached into a meshed meat safe and produced a thin, bloody strip of steak.

'Thanks,' said Farrell, 'but I really ain't hungry.'

'No, no,' said Lee. 'Not to eat. For medicine.'

Before Farrell could protest, Lee had plastered the dripping meat against his left eye which had become badly cut and swollen.

'You hold it there real tight.'

Farrell subsided on to a bench, obediently clutching the steak to his face as Lee busied himself over the stove.

'Here, Mr Matt,' said Lee, thrusting a steaming mug of coffee into his unoccupied hand. 'This do you good too. I made it extra strong. You sit there and take your time. Boss just sent Mr Frank into town with Miss Hetty so he won't come bothering you. This is big ranch but you are two big men – not much room for both of you.'

'Right.'

The coffee was too hot to drink, but Farrell sat with his eyes closed inhaling the aroma, while he slowly got his brain back into working order. Lee prattled on, evidently glad to have a captive audience for once, and apparently unconcerned that the conversation was entirely one-sided. At length Farrell drained his mug and stood up.

'Thanks, Lee. You made me a new man.'

He dropped the strip of steak back on to the chopping table.

'It's OK, Mr Matt, you hold on to the steak. It keep working all afternoon. Then maybe I broil it for you tonight.'

Farrell shook his head.

'I got things to do – it'd be in my way.'

He turned to go. His head was quite clear now, and something the cook had said had brought his thoughts sharply into focus. It looked like being a busy Sunday.

NINE

Hetty Ferguson drummed the ferrule of her parasol on the tile floor of the porch and directed a baleful glance at her father, who was leaning against the stone balustrade. 'Really, Pa. You can be quite provoking at times.'

'Yeah?'

'Yes, quite. First you won't let me drive myself into town, then you lumber me with McCoy's company, of all people.'

'Don't see what the problem is. Frank's reliable.'

'So are most of the hands. Why couldn't you have picked—'

'Because it was the easiest way to keep the peace. If McCoy's been fighting, a couple of hours away from the ranch will give time for tempers to cool. Seems quite logical to me, even if it don't quite suit you, missy.'

Hetty pursed her lips, reluctant to let her father have the last word on the issue of her escort. But before she could frame an adequate riposte the crunching of wheels on gravel announced the arrival of the surrey. Frank McCoy jumped down and came up to the porch.

'Sorry to keep you waiting, Miss Hetty.'

He snatched off his hat as Hetty stepped past him without a word and followed her to the carriage. Ignoring the hand he proffered to help her up, she clambered aboard – with some difficulty, as she had to manage her skirts, the parasol and the reticule in which was tucked an extra large contribution for the church collection. McCoy climbed up beside her, flicked the reins and set the horses into a sedate trot. The first few minutes of the drive were accomplished in total silence. But at length, when they were well clear of the ranch, McCoy checked the pace of the horses and turned to his passenger.

'Everything all right, Miss Hetty?'

'Perfectly, thank you,' she replied, looking steadily ahead. 'Why shouldn't it be?'

'Oh, nothing. It's just that you seem a bit quiet.'

When Hetty failed to respond, he continued, 'You angry about something?'

'Of course not. Why should I be.'

'Oh, I don't know. I mean . . . being kept waiting and all. . . .'

There was a further silence as Hetty again failed to respond, and then McCoy tried again.

'Kind of an exciting time in town last night. You hear about it?'

'Something.'

He glanced across at her. Her face was a study in feigned lack of interest, but McCoy continued unabashed and gave her a bare account of the previous night's events.

'Reckon the kid got what was coming to him,' McCoy concluded. 'Of course, if Farrell hadn't bust him out, he would have ended up with a rope round his neck anyway, the way folks were feeling.'

Hetty pursed her lips.

'Can't see why they got so excited that they had to take the law into their own hands. Surely they ought to have known they could leave it to Sheriff Finch. They've known him long enough.'

'Time of day, maybe,' said McCoy with a shrug.

'Saturday nights people are always looking for a bit of entertainment.'

'Entertainment? Since when has stringing someone up been entertainment around here? I'll be interested to hear what Reverend Fletcher has to say about it all in his sermon this morning. If anyone's got the brass face to turn up at church and be lectured, that is.'

The tone of disgust in Hetty's voice was so marked that McCoy fell silent. They were now a mile or so from town, and the road was leading down from a stretch of low sandy hills to where a green spread of shrubs and cottonwood trees marked the course of the Pine river. The road levelled out and began to run through the shade of the wooded area with the river directly to one side. As they reached a glade where the ferns and shrubbery cleared to give a picturesque view of the watercourse, McCoy eased the horses to a stop.

'Something wrong?' asked Hetty with a frown.

'Left hander might be runnin' a tad lame,' muttered McCoy. He clambered down and addressed himself to the left hand horse, carefully lifting its hoofs one by one and examining the plates. After making a few perfunctory adjustments to the horse's left front hoof, he straightened up and returned to join Hetty on the leather front bench.

'Thought it might have cast a shoe, but it was only a stone got lodged underneath.'

He took up the reins, hesitated, and then laid them down again. He leant against the backrest with his arm tentatively stretched towards her along the top of the seat.

'Miss Hetty,' he began, 'you mentioning church just now put me in mind of something I been meaning to ask you.'

'Ask me? Ask me what?'

Undeterred by the note of frosty puzzlement in her voice, McCoy stumbled on, as if afraid that his words – or his courage – might suddenly dry up.

'Ask . . . ask about us . . .'

'About us? What on earth do you mean?'

'Well, Miss Hetty, I mean . . . we've known each other a long time. I know you and you know me, so it ain't as if we're not well acquainted.'

'Kind of stating the obvious, aren't you?'

'Maybe, maybe not. But what I'm coming to is that you're of marriageable age, and I've kind of reached the time of life when a man gets to thinking about settling down properly and—'

'Frank McCoy,' cut in Hetty, before he could get his sentence out. 'Are you proposing to me?'

With a sigh suggesting relief that she had saved him the embarrassment of fully articulating his thoughts, McCoy edged himself a little further towards her on the bench.

'Well that's just it, ma'am. I mean, you know I'm no two-bit cowboy. I know the ranching business inside out. We could easily . . .'

Hetty shook her head in bewilderment.

'But there's no question . . .'

'And it needn't be a question of money,' he continued eagerly, 'if that's what's bothering you. I got more than you might imagine. Seems to me that with all the cattle-raising land around these parts, between us we could create one of the biggest spreads in the territory. What do you say?'

Oblivious to the look of frozen distaste on her face he grabbed her upper arm in a clumsy attempt to draw her closer to him.

'What I say,' she replied, wrenching her arm away from his grasp, 'is that you must be out of your mind. What on earth gives you the idea that I'm thinking of entering into matrimony with anybody, let alone you.'

'But you're growed up now,' he persisted. 'Stands to reason you need to start looking. That's what I mean about us being a match. You got me ready made, as it were. And I don't reckon as your pa would object, if I put it to him as a serious proposition, man to man.'

'Now you're making it sound like a business deal.'

'Well, I wouldn't put it like that. But most marriages around these parts is made with an eye to the future. I guess your pa would see it along those lines too.'

'Maybe he would. But I can assure you I don't. I wouldn't consider marrying you even if you owned half the county. And there's a simple reason. I'm not in love with you, and I doubt I ever could be.'

'But surely you feel—'

'Nothing,' snapped Hetty. She reached across, snatched up the reins and flipped the horses into action. 'And I've had quite enough of this conversation. Now would you kindly take charge of these critters and get me into town? We're running late enough as it is.'

With beads of sweat coursing down his bruised face, and crimson with humiliation, McCoy cracked the whip viciously over the horses' heads to set the surrey bouncing hell for leather along the road regardless of comfort or even safety. They completed the rest of the journey as they had begun it – in total silence – and McCoy only checked the pace as they entered Main Street. Having driven through town and up the lane to where various members of the church congregation were assembling in their Sunday best, McCoy handed Hetty down from the surrey.

'Are you joining me?' she enquired in a voice which clearly anticipated a negative reply.

McCoy shook his head with lowered eyes.

'I'll wait here.'

With no further word Hetty turned away towards the church, greeting various acquaintances to left and right as McCoy slouched morosely against the carriage. Then he glanced up at the steeple clock and stirred himself into action. Consigning the surrey and its equipage to the temporary care of another ranch hand who was engaged on a similar watching brief he dug his hands deep into his pockets and wandered over to the premises which until yesterday had been the Pinedale Travellers Temperance Hotel.

Pushing his way through the glass doors he paused on the threshold to take in the new décor and furnishings of the lobby, and then strode over to the reception desk. The young man on duty, a hangover from the previous regime, nodded politely.

'Morning, Frank. Something I can do for you?'

'Fellow still get a cup of coffee around here under the new management?'

'Sure.' The receptionist smiled and then inclined his head towards the connecting door to the saloon. 'But the bar's open next door, if you fancy something stronger.'

'I sure as hell need it. But best not. I'm driving Miss Hetty back to the ranch in an hour. She won't appreciate the smell of whiskey on my breath.'

'That's women for you.'

'Too right,' acknowledged McCoy, with a grimace.

He turned round, selected a comfortable armchair near the fireplace and propped his boots up on the fender. After a few minutes the receptionist reappeared with a tray of coffee which he set down on an adjacent table.

'There you go. Brought you some reading material to pass the time.'

He dropped a folded newspaper beside the tray and withdrew to the reception desk. McCoy poured himself some coffee and stared moodily at the unlit logs in the fireplace. He had just finished his second cup when the clock on the mantelshelf struck the quarter before noon. He sighed, stretched and stood up. As he pushed his chair

124

back the armrest dislodged the newspaper which had lain folded and unnoticed during his period of silent meditation. He bent over to retrieve it and as he picked it up it fell open at the front page. McCoy stared at it for a moment. Then he frowned and tucked it unobtrusively under his arm. He dropped a few coins on the table in settlement for the coffee, walked out of the hotel and retraced his steps to the surrey. He manoeuvred the horses round to face Main Street, and had just completed the operation when the church doors opened and the congregation filed out. With Miss Hetty once again on board McCoy started the carriage moving with such determination that the jolt shoved the backrest sharply into her spine.

'Kind of in a hurry, aren't we?' she commented, holding on to her bonnet.

McCoy made no reply, but immediately set the horses into a pace which was clearly designed to allow no further opportunity either for conversation or for admiring the scenery.

Farrell walked back to the bunkhouse, scraped the dust and mud from the corral off his boots and then made his way over to the ranch house. He climbed the steps to the porch, hesitated for a moment and then pulled on the bell. After a few moments the front door was opened by the maid.

'Boss in?'

Rosa nodded, held open the door and pointed him in the direction of the study. Ferguson looked up from the papers on his desk as Farrell tapped at the doorframe.

'Mind if I see you for a moment?'

Ferguson studied him carefully for a few seconds.

'All right.'

Farrell advanced towards the desk and paused, turning

his hat awkwardly in his hands.

'I just came to tell you I'm quitting.'

Ferguson's face remained expressionless.

'OK. I hear you and McCoy have been fighting. Anything to do with that?'

'I guess so.'

'You guess so. Don't seem very positive about it. Seems to me a fellow should always know why he's quitting a job.'

'Well . . . fact is I haven't got a choice.'

'That so? Why, did McCoy whip you?'

'Not exactly, but . . .'

'So did you whip McCoy? Story's going round that you gave him a real good licking.' Farrell scratched his head, bewildered at the rapid, and apparently uncontrollable, circulation of a bunkhouse myth.

'Not exactly that, either. But the fact is, it was sort of a fight to the death – even if both of us were left standing. And as he's still standing there ain't no room for me around here any longer.'

Ferguson pondered this explanation for a moment and then nodded.

'Can't quibble with your thinking. Kind of a pity to lose a man with your abilities, but if you can't make out with my foreman you'd be wasting your time here. You told him the good news?'

'Nope. You sent him into town. That's why I'm telling you.'

'All right. You owe me a week's notice of course, so we'll—'

'Notice? I was kind of figuring on quitting right now, if it's all the same to you. Like I said . . .'

'That urgent, huh? OK, best grab your saddle-roll and skedaddle.'

Ferguson dropped his head and resumed his perusal of the papers on his desk. Slightly taken aback by the abrupt

126

termination of the interview Farrell hesitated and then turned on his heel. As he was at the door Ferguson suddenly spoke again.

'This ... er ... difference of opinion with McCoy. It wasn't over a woman, was it?'

Farrell faced him with a frown.

'Why no. We just didn't ...'

'All right. Just curious.'

Farrell turned again, and made his way out of the house, pondering Ferguson's last question. As he saw it, this morning's fight had been provoked by McCoy's gibes about his masculinity. But behind it there lay the indisputable fact that McCoy's hostility was derived from something deeper. And the old man's question seemed to suggest that he was aware of that something. Or had it just been a shot in the dark?

Oh, well ... it was irrelevant now. The reality was, that there was no way that he and McCoy could co-exist on the same ranch – and since he had failed to defeat McCoy in the ring the foreman remained a fixture while Farrell was eminently dispensable. Ferguson had grasped the point without difficulty, which was why he had made no bones about Farrell leaving. Ranches were unsentimental places and that was a fact of life. Filled with self-reproach at the turn of events Farrell made his way back to the bunkhouse to collect his few belongings. Lee was there, in his alternative role as master magician of the washhouse, distributing freshly laundered shirts from a large wicker basket to the various bunks.

'Nice timing, Lee,' grunted Farrell. 'I'm about to pack.'

'What?'

'I just quit.'

'Oh, that real bad, Mr Matt. Why you not stay?'

'Ranch ain't big enough for me and McCoy. Time to make myself scarce.'

'We miss you. Where you going?'

'Wherever,' replied Farrell with a note of irritation in his voice. He hadn't the faintest idea which way to head. 'Look, just gimme my shirts, will you.'

'Sure.'

Lee rummaged in the basket and dropped three shirts on Farrell's bunk.

'Thanks,' said Farrell, fingering the laundry. And then: 'Hey, the blue one's not mine.'

Lee stepped over to inspect the rogue item.

'Sorry, Mr Matt. That one belong Mr Frank.' Lee picked up the shirt and shook his head. 'I'll put it at the bottom of his pile. He won't be too pleased I couldn't get the cuff clean. Blood isn't always that easy.'

'Blood?'

'Sure. Look.'

Lee held up the cuff of the right sleeve where blackish stains were visible round the edge. Farrell's eyes narrowed as he viewed the imperfectly laundered exhibit, but he made no comment. When Lee had finished his distribution and left, Farrell sat down on his bunk, with all thoughts of packing his saddle-roll temporarily banished. The sight of McCoy's shirt had suddenly brought back the events of the previous night into sharper focus. He had been quite genuine in his reluctance to acquiesce in Finch's suggestion that he act as unpaid snooper in the investigation of the death of Beth Carney's brother. And of course the discussion had been suddenly overtaken and blotted out by the unexpected eruption of the lynch mob. He and McCoy might be at loggerheads, but the law was Finch's business and no place for amateurs. At least, that was how he had viewed it last night. But against his gut instincts not to involve himself, the sight of that blood-stained cuff had suddenly set his mind racing. Stained shirts were no uncommon sight on the average cattle ranch. The work was rough and the men were always cutting themselves up on ropes or fencing. But Farrell had just seen McCoy stripped to the waist in the corral, and he was quite sure that until the damage inflicted in the course of their fight, McCoy's bare torso and arms were completely unmarked. Whoever's blood was on that shirt, it wasn't McCoy's.

Farrell sat on his bunk in an agony of indecision. On the one hand, having given in his notice, he was anxious to put distance between himself and the ranch without further delay. On the other, his curiosity was aroused by the sudden falling into place of a piece of evidence that appeared to corroborate what last night had only been speculation and conjecture. He stared about him. McCoy was safely out of the way, and the bunkhouse was deserted as the men went about their Sunday morning duties. If he was going to act as Finch's proxy there would never be a better moment. At length Farrell stood up, resolved that the situation could not be ducked.

As foreman, McCoy had the privilege of a room to himself. In practice it was nothing more than an area partitioned off from the far end of the bunkhouse, affording a bit of privacy but little else. Farrell walked across and eased open the door. The space contained just a bunk and a chest of drawers above which McCoy's prized Winchester rifle was fixed in a couple of brackets. The freshly laundered shirts which Lee had just brought in were laid out on the counterpane. McCoy's shaving-tackle and a few other personal items were arranged neatly on the chest of drawers, but otherwise the cubicle was bare.

With little hope of finding anything Farrell eased open the drawers one by one and fingered his way gingerly through the contents, taking care not to disturb anything. He found nothing but clothes. He turned to the bed and eased the mattress off its timber frame, but there was nothing concealed underneath. Farrell dropped the mattress back into place with a faint sensation of self-disgust. He had no regard for McCoy, but raking through a guy's pitiful personal possessions scarcely seemed the act of a hero. In fact it ran directly counter to the informal convention that within the closely confined living conditions of the bunkhouse you treated a man and his possessions with respect.

Farrell grimaced and brought his search to a conclusion. Barring the possibility of something being hidden beneath the floorboards – and there was certainly no sign that they had been recently disturbed – the only other unexamined space was under the bunk frame. Farrell knelt down. The only thing to meet his eye was a carpet-bag which had been stuffed under one end. Farrell carefully eased it out and peered inside, but the contents were a disappointment: only a few trinkets and personal letters.

He was about to push it back when he noticed another object which had been lying underneath the bag. He drew out a set of leather saddle-pouches which had been spread nearly flat and pushed against the boards of the partition wall against which the bunk was set. Farrell flipped open the straps on one of the pouches. The interior was stuffed with greenbacks. Farrell didn't even bother to pull out all the money and count it. There was clearly more here than any ranch foreman could possibly put by in the way of savings even after a lifetime of hard work.

At first sight it seemed extraordinary that McCoy should have left the proceeds of his crime so inadequately protected, but as Farrell reflected on the situation he concluded that maybe it was less surprising. First, although there were plenty of more secure places of concealment McCoy probably hadn't yet had time to arrange anything. His encounter with Beth's brother had only taken place a couple of days ago, and the murder and robbery had probably not been premeditated, so nothing would have been prepared in advance. Secondly, McCoy had probably felt that he was safe in relying on the established custom that his privacy would be respected. In the ordinary run of events his room would be quite undisturbed – and of course there was no reason for any of the hands to think he had anything worth stealing. He could scarcely have anticipated that anyone would make the connection between himself and the dead man so quickly. Having worked all this out, Farrell sat back on his heels and considered what to do next.

Sunday mornings were always quiet in Pinedale Fork, but this particular morning the town seemed to have a slightly hangdog air about it – as though the citizenry were in a state of repentance for their behaviour of the night before. At least, that was the impression that Farrell had as he cantered his horse into Main Street. When he reached the sheriff's office he paused to survey the evidence of last night's violence and then wheeled over towards the hitching rail and dismounted. The town might have made a late start, but Finch had evidently been busy. A pair of carpenters and glaziers supplied by Joe Doyle were hard at work making emergency repairs to the damaged windows and door.

'Sheriff at home?' enquired Farrell. When one of the men nodded, Farrell pushed his way inside. Finch was sprawled at his desk tidying papers, while Clem Parker was busy with a dustpan and broom clearing up the splinters of glass and timber that were strewn all over the floor.

'Ain't open for business,' grunted Finch, without looking up.

'Yeah?' enquired Farrell, gesturing towards one of the partially glazed windows. 'Seems like you're more open than usual.'

'Oh, it's you.' Finch stopped riffling his papers. 'Pull up a chair, if you can find one that isn't broken.'

'I'll stand.'

'Suit yourself.' Finch leaned back to survey his visitor. 'Guess I ought to thank you for what you did last night. In all the confusion, I never got round to it. Didn't realize you'd got your face whacked for your trouble.'

'Oh,' said Farrell, rubbing his swollen eye, 'that wasn't anything to do with it. And anyway, I didn't do much. Kid ended up dead in any case. I don't call that much of a result.'

'Whatever. You tried. And it wasn't your fault he took a header.'

Farrell scowled. If he'd taken the trouble to find out the location of Miss Beth's bedroom before he bust the kid out, maybe they could have ridden things out till the morning without McCoy bursting in and upsetting the applecart. He opened his mouth to give vent to his misgivings, but then thought better of it. What had happened had happened and there was nothing to be gained from recriminations. He edged closer to the desk and then spoke in a tone low enough to be inaudible to the men working at the window.

'As a matter of fact, I rode in on another matter of business.'

'Oh?' said Finch, staring at him blankly.

'Yeah. You know . . . that other matter we were discussing with Mizz Beth before things kinda got out of control.'

'Right,' nodded Finch. 'So you've been thinking it over, huh?'

'In a manner of speaking. Both before and after I found the money.'

Finch's eyes opened wide as he stood up abruptly.

132

'OK, Clem,' he said, turning to his assistant. 'Looks tidy enough in here. Why don't you clean up out front. Guess Doyle's men are just about finished.'

He waited until they were alone and then continued: 'Son-of-a-gun. You don't waste any time, do you, Farrell? Well, don't just stand there – spit it out.'

Farrell gave him an account of what had happened at the ranch that morning. When he had finished Finch permitted himself a grunt of satisfaction.

'Smart thinking, and smart work. You ever considered putting on a lawman's badge? There's kind of a shortage of men who can handle themselves the way you can.'

'If that's an offer of a job you can forget it. I thought I made myself clear last night.'

'All right. Well, hand over the money. If McCoy's still at the church with Miss Hetty I guess I can take things along from here and bring him straight in.'

Farrell looked blank. 'I haven't got the money.'

'What in tarnation are you talking about? You just said you found it.'

'Sure. And I put it right back where McCoy had hidden it.'

'You put it back?' muttered Finch, scratching his head in bewilderment. 'But—'

'Look,' said Farrell suddenly exasperated by the apparent slowness of Finch's thought processes. 'To nail McCoy you've got to catch him red-handed with the money, right? No point in me just turning up with it. I could just as easily have knocked off Beth's brother myself. As you're so fond of saying, *the man who finds the body generally did the crime.*'

Finch held his arms up in mock surrender.

'All right, you shot me with my own quote. Like I said, you think real smart.'

Finch hitched up his pants and summoned Parker from his sweeping duties.

133

'Saddle up. We're riding out to Ferguson's with Mr Farrell here on business.'

'With me?' queried Farrell. 'Sheriff, you ain't been listening too good. I already told you that I quit the ranch. I've done my bit for you, Mizz Beth and the law in general. Now I'm riding out.'

Before Finch could adduce any arguments for his further involvement he made for the door. As he reached it, however, he suddenly checked himself in mid-stride and clamped his hand to his forehead.

'Jesus, I'm a bonehead.'

'Something wrong?' enquired Finch.

'Nothing,' replied Farrell with a wry smile. 'Except that in my hurry to ride over here to give you the good news I clean forgot to pack my saddle-roll. Seems like I got to go back to the ranch, anyway.'

Finch chuckled.

'Attaboy. Makes perfect sense to me.'

TEN

'That horse of yours go any faster, Sheriff?'

Jade Finch glanced across at the impatient expression on Farrell's face, adjusted the angle of his wide-brimmed hat but made no alteration to the spine-jarring jog-trot which he had insisted on maintaining all the way from Pinedale Fork.

'My, you young men are always in a hurry. No sense in sweating up the horses.'

'Sure. We got all the time in the world.'

Ignoring the heavy note of irony in Farrell's voice, Finch nodded in apparent agreement.

'McCoy don't know we're on to him so he won't be expecting us to come calling.'

Farrell gritted his teeth. Finch was right, of course, but it didn't make the slow reaction of the law any easier to stomach – especially when you were fixed on getting on with your life as far away from Pinedale Fork as possible. Matters had proceeded at a snail's pace ever since he had agreed to ride back to the ranch. First Parker had been dispatched to establish whether McCoy had left with Miss Hetty. Then, when he returned to report in the affirmative, more time had been wasted in an earnest discussion about the precise level of armaments that would be appropriate to the intended arrest, six-shooters and one Winchester being finally agreed on.

135

So it was well after noon before the three of them set out. And it would, Farrell reckoned, be a full hour at the present rate before they reached the ranch. The horses might be fresh and unsweated, but Farrell could feel himself lathering up – more from frustration than the effects of the blistering early afternoon sun. Resisting the temptation to dig in his spurs and set his own pace, Farrell set his jaw and endured both the ride and Finch's ruminations and occasional nuggets of homespun philosophy, none of which, as far as he could see, had much to do with the case in hand.

At length the familiar pastures of the Ferguson ranch hove into sight, and the three men proceeded along the track that led up to the ranch house. Old man Ferguson was standing on the porch staring at the approaching riders. They pulled up beside the surrey which was slewed awkwardly across the path as if having been parked in haste. Before they had time to dismount Ferguson had stumped down the steps and positioned himself in front of Finch's horse with a thunderous expression on his face. 'Will somebody tell me what in tarnation's going on around here? First Farrell here quits, takes off like a bat out of hell and then turns up again. Then my daughter turns up from a ride to church all in a bother about some unwelcome attention from my foreman. Then McCoy lights out of here with scarcely a by-your-leave after god-knows-how-many years of service. I gotta business to run here, and if—'

'Hey, hey, wait a minute,' interrupted Finch with his hand raised to stem the flow of invective. 'Hold it a minute, Mr Ferguson. You're saying McCoy left—'

'I'm saying McCoy came back here, bounced into my parlour without so much as knocking, told me he was quitting – and then did exactly that. No explanation, no notice, no warning. Never had such a Sunday morning in

136

my life. And if all this,' he continued, turning towards Farrell, 'is your doing, I'm gonna bust your hide, mister.' With more agility than Farrell would have given him credit for on the basis of recent performance Finch swung himself down from his horse so as to interpose himself between Farrell and his erstwhile employer.

'It is to do with Farrell in a manner of speaking, but it ain't his fault. I rode up here with the aim of arresting McCoy, but it seems he's anticipated me.'

'Arresting him? What in tarnation for?'

'Murder and handling stolen property.'

Ferguson chewed this information over for a moment, and then mopped his overheated brow with his shirtcuff.

'You'd better come inside.'

They trooped into the house, where it took a few minutes for Finch to explain the situation. When he had finished, Ferguson scratched his head in puzzlement.

'All right, so McCoy's a wanted man. But like you say, he didn't know you were on to him. So what made him vamoose in such a hurry?'

Finch shrugged. 'Something must have spooked him. But one thing's sure. However fast he moved, the money went with him.' He turned to Farrell. 'I suppose we'd better go and verify my suspicions.'

Farrell led the way across to the bunkhouse outside which a number of the hands had clustered in curiosity at the sudden burst of activity. The three men squeezed into McCoy's cubicle which showed every sign of having been evacuated in haste. The chest of drawers had been pulled open and emptied, McCoy's small collection of personal effects, including his rifle, had disappeared – and of course, when Farrell explored under the bunk, the saddle-pouches had gone. He stood up, crimson-faced.

'Looks like I just lost you several thousand dollars. If I'd only brought it into town at least . . .'

137

'Yeah,' said Finch. 'At least we'd have the money, if not the man.'

He turned to Parker who was standing in the doorway behind them. 'Looks like there's a long afternoon ahead of the two of us, pardy.'

'The two of you. . . ?' began Farrell.

'Sure. We got a chase on our hands now.'

'Make it three,' corrected Farrell, grimly staring down at the empty space under the bunk. 'This affair finally got personal.'

They returned to the house where Ferguson was resting against the side of the abandoned surrey.

'Yep,' said Finch. 'He took the cash right enough. How much of a start has he got on us?'

Ferguson pursed his lips.

'Anywhere up to an hour I guess. But at least I know what spooked him. Look,' he gestured towards the newspaper which was spread open on the front seat of the carriage, 'just found that lying on the floor.'

Peering over, Farrell recognized the same article that Beth Carney had spotted the night before.

'Reckon he figured that someone would connect the names quick enough – if they hadn't done so already,' said Ferguson. 'Pity you took so long to get here.'

'More haste, less speed,' said Finch, looking blandly across at Farrell.

But there was a further delay – this time at Farrell's insistence. His horse had already covered more than six miles, and if there was going to be a prolonged chase he wanted a completely fresh mount. With Ferguson's consent he selected the best available horse from the corral, saddled it up and joined the other two men. They cantered briskly down the track until they reached the main trail.

'No problem guessing which way he went,' grunted

Finch as they reined in their horses. 'He didn't come head to head with us on the way out, so he must have . . .' He gestured leftwards to where the trail led south.

'Stands to reason,' said Farrell. 'There's less than thirty miles between here and Mexico.'

'Son-of-a . . .' spat Finch. It was the first time that Farrell had seen him really animated.

The sheriff dug in his spurs and led the way down the trail at a dust-raising gallop. That, thought Farrell, as he charged after him, was a first too.

The trail, which was well beaten out by the stagecoaches that plied regularly down to the border, was easy enough to follow. The breakneck pace which Finch had set initially was soon eased to a more sustainable canter, and after some twenty minutes of silent riding Finch checked his companions to allow the horses a breather.

'Of course, he could have struck across country,' he said as the other two riders came abreast.

'Except that he's no reason to,' said Farrell, 'if he doesn't think anyone's close on his heels. Trail's the straightest route to the border. And anyway he can't make it in one ride. Even if he doesn't need to rest, his horse does – unless he changes it. Either way he needs to stop somewhere. That means staying on the trail.'

Farrell's conjecture proved correct a few minutes later when they reached a straggling hamlet consisting of nothing more than a few homesteads scattered on either side of the trail. A ragged boy volunteered the information that a rider conforming to McCoy's description had stopped to water his horse some time previously, but was annoyingly vague about how long it was since he had passed through. Less than an hour he thought. Maybe.

'Damn useless kid,' muttered Finch as they rode on.

'But at least we know McCoy's out there ahead of us some-where.'

He turned in his saddle to address Parker.

'Hey, Clem. You know these parts better than me. What's between here and the border?'

'Cactus, sagebrush and hell of a lot of dirt.'

'Yeah, I know that, muttonhead. I mean any townships?'

Clem chewed his lips.

'Mesquite Creek about ten miles from the border. Next place up from here is . . .' Clem paused to scratch his head. '. . . High Stakes.'

'High what?' queried Farrell.

'High Stakes,' said Clem. 'Kind of a joke. Few years ago some diggers thought they'd hit a turquoise seam like the ones they got in New Mexico. So they staked it out. Didn't come to anything, though. More dust than fancy jewellery. Don't reckon McCoy'll find anything worth stopping for in that ghost town.'

They rode on in silence. Farrell kept wondering how much ground they had made up on the fugitive, but he was not kept in suspense for much longer. The trail dipped down through a defile which led to a wooded area surrounding a creek. As the path levelled out and they rounded an outcrop of boulders the figure of a man stand-ing beside a browsing horse was visible some two or three hundred yards distant.

'That's him,' grunted Finch pointing ahead.

McCoy spotted the three men at almost exactly the same moment that they spotted him. He raised his hand to shield his eyes from the sunlight that was filtering through the foliage and stood immobile for a few seconds. If there was any lingering doubt about whether McCoy recognized his pursuers or whether he knew the purpose of their pursuit his next action dispelled it. He ran to his horse, extracted his rifle, levelled it at the oncoming riders and fired. Before the crack of the shot reached Farrell's ears the bullet had already zipped between him and Finch, slicing across the crown of the sheriff's hat and sending it skimming to the ground. With an oath Finch clutched the side of his head and fell sideways off his horse.

Farrell and Clem mechanically loosed off some retaliatory shots at the distant figure with their six-shooters, but the range was hopeless. They watched McCoy mount and gallop off. However, before they could follow, it was necessary to give some attention to Finch. Farrell dismounted and knelt beside him. The bullet had grazed sheer across one side of the sheriff's head, removing skin and hair in a straight line. Blood was trickling down the side of his face.

'Jesus, he almost scalped you,' muttered Farrell.

'I'm all right,' gasped Finch, struggling to his feet. 'Skunk fair took me by surprise.' He fished in his pocket and produced a large handkerchief which he folded and pressed to the wound to stanch the bleeding. Then he rammed his tattered hat down on top to keep the temporary bandage in place. 'Come on, let's get after him. We know he ain't far ahead now.'

With McCoy so close there was no point in sparing the horses. They jabbed them into a gallop and careered off along the trail. Having descended to the creek the track now started to rise, weaving its way up and through a series of bare sandy hills. Clouds of dust which had barely had time to settle indicated that McCoy was only minutes ahead of them.

After a few minutes they crested the top of a ridge and found themselves looking down into a shallow valley. The trail wound away into the distance, but less than half a mile ahead of them lay a scattered collection of clapboard sheds and primitive adobe huts.

'High Stakes,' said Clem.

His comment was superfluous, because as Finch

141

checked their pace with a wave of his hand Farrell found himself staring at a wooden sign which had been posted by the side of the road. Burnt into the timber with a poker or branding iron the legend read: *High Stakes – low profits.* Immediately underneath, some departing wit had additionally inscribed *Pop. 000.*

As the others reined in beside him Finch pointed to where the trail continued towards the horizon beyond the deserted township.

'You see any dust raised over there?'

'Nope,' said Farrell. 'Which means . . .'

'. . . the varmint's gone to ground somewhere in that collection of deadwood.'

Finch chewed his lip as he appraised the situation.

'Well,' he said, after a moment's thought. 'The good news is that we're three to one against him, and as well armed. The not so good news is that he's not going to be easy to winkle out of there if he cares to make a fight of it. At the moment we're out of range of that rifle of his, but if we ride straight in we'll be sitting ducks. He can pick us off one at a time.'

'Seems to me,' said Farrell, 'that we'd do best to split up and circle around. He can't point that rifle in three directions at once. We need to pin him down and then smoke him out. Once we know where he is we can close in.'

As Parker nodded his assent Finch made up his mind.

'OK. Let's get to it while we still got plenty of daylight.'

He led them to a clump of trees some 500 yards from the nearest of the wooden buildings – which was as close as he was prepared to risk on horseback. They dismounted and tethered the horses. Finch slipped the rifle out of its holster and surveyed the scene of operations. The trail cut a wide swathe through the scattered sheds – presumably having formed a sort of Main Street during the brief era of the township's commercial operations. At the moment they had no idea which side of the street McCoy had positioned himself on. There was no sign of his horse, either.

'You sure he's here?' murmured Farrell.

'Positive. We had clear view of the trail from up back there. He wasn't on it.'

'So what now?'

'We get in closer of course. You and Clem stay this side of the trail and work your way separately round the back of the buildings. I'll take the other side and work my way along until I'm level with you.'

Tucking the rifle under his arm Finch crouched down, edged his way to the side of the road, scuttled across and then hurled himself flat into the gravel. Farrell held his breath during this brief manoeuvre. If McCoy had them in his sights Finch was totally exposed for a few seconds, but there was no shot. They were just about out of effective range, and McCoy no doubt knew it. Anyway at this stage he would probably be too canny to give his position away.

The intervening terrain between themselves and the first of the buildings was devoid of cover except for low scrub and thorn bushes. This made any further approach on horseback impossible, but the vegetation provided just enough of a screen to enable Farrell and Parker to worm their way forward, alternately crouching and slithering across the stony ground. Even so, Farrell's head felt uncomfortably exposed, and he could feel the hairs on the nape of his neck prickling with the danger of their advance. When they had reached the first of the buildings Farrell waved his arm to send Parker inching his way round the back to the further end of the street.

As Parker disappeared Farrell removed his hat and inched forward to the edge of the trail. From here, even with his chin in the dust, he at last had a close up view of the ghost town. A random collection of abandoned clapboard sheds stretched away southwards. One or two even possessed the remnants of fascia boards proclaiming their original function such as STORE and SALOON. Interspersed with these were a few crumbling adobe huts which might have been part of an earlier Indian settlement. A stiff breeze was constantly teasing and rattling the rotten timbers and glassless window frames, while the lowering sun in the western sky was beginning to cast long shadows. Even without the menacing presence of McCoy the effect would have been decidedly sinister, and despite the continuing heat of the afternoon Farrell found himself shivering.

He lay motionless for a minute or so scanning the area across the street for any sign of Finch's approach. At length a slight disturbance of the thicket a hundred yards or so across from him indicated that the sheriff was closing up. He watched as Finch wriggled his way forward to the edge of the first shed on the other side of the street so that they were almost facing each other. Farrell had no idea what to do next, but Finch took the initiative.

'We know you're in there, McCoy,' he yelled. 'You saw you're outnumbered, so throw down that rifle and come out with your hands up. We won't shoot.'

Finch's words echoed round the deserted street, but there was no response. When he spoke again it was to hiss an instruction across to Farrell.

'Cover me. I'm goin' forward.'

Farrell unholstered his Colt and levelled it vaguely up the street while Finch straightened himself and rushed over the bare ground to reach the porch of the nearest building. Then he edged himself across the creaking boards to the empty doorframe. He sprang forward to reach the interior, but as he did so Farrell spotted the sudden glint of sunlight on metal from behind a balustrade further along the same side of the street. Before Finch could reach safety a shot had rung out and

144

the sheriff collapsed to the boards with a yell of pain. Farrell fired a couple of covering shots in the direction of where he supposed McCoy to be – not with any hope of hitting a target but to prevent him getting a second shot at Finch who was now lying flat out, wounded evidently, but still alive. At the same time he saw Parker take his opportunity to scuttle out of cover further down and cross to the same side of the street as McCoy.

'You all right, Sheriff?' he called hopefully across to the prostrate figure.

'Took a whack in my leg, but I'll be OK.'

Finch wriggled himself into a more comfortable position and trained his rifle down the street.

'Listen,' he continued. 'I can pin him to this side of the street now we know where he is. I'll count three and loose off a shot to make him put his head down. When I do, you scuttle across here and work your way round behind him.'

There was a pause as Farrell gathered himself for the dash, and then Finch signalled the count. There was a flash and a sharp report as he unleashed a shot down the street, while Farrell bolted like a startled hare across to where Finch was lying. A vicious retaliatory shot whanged into the timbers somewhere above his head, sending a cascade of dry splinters down to the floorboards.

'We got him, Farrell,' muttered Finch, keeping his eyes and the rifle trained down the street. 'I just see Clem cross the street. If you both get behind McCoy I can cut off any escape up or down the trail.'

'Yeah, but—'

'Don't give me any buts. Get your ass out of here and smoke him out.'

Keeping his belly on the ground Farrell reversed direction and edged his way back to the corner of the building without attracting any further fire. Once around the corner he stood up cautiously and made his way to the back. A miscellaneous collection of ruined outbuildings dotted the route southwards. Farrell spent a sweaty five minutes tacking and weaving from one to the other trying to get himself approximately level to where he guessed McCoy had been shooting from. There was no sound of any further action elsewhere, but this made him even more suspicious. Had McCoy taken the opportunity of the lull to shift his vantage point? And where was Parker? The sense of imminent danger was acute, but circumstances were working against him. The persistent breeze was blowing dust and tumbleweed in all directions and constantly worrying at loose boards and shutters, causing them to creak and flap. With the constant background noise and movement confusing the senses it was very difficult to pinpoint what was relevant and what could be safely ignored.

He was just cursing all this, when he became aware of one particular sound that surely had nothing to do with the desert wind. It was the faint but unmistakable snorting of a horse. Since their own mounts were tethered over a quarter of a mile away Farrell knew that he must be hearing McCoy's horse. But where was it? He glanced around but could see no sign of it. Holding his breath he waited for the next sound. Then, just for a moment, the wind died down and he heard the animal again. This time the sound was clearly coming from a shed some twenty yards to his right. His first thought was that the horse might be snorting in response to its master's presence. Could McCoy have slipped over there with the intention of riding out, in the knowledge that it would take his pursuers at least five minutes to recover their own mounts? There was only one way to find out.

Keeping close to the ground he scuttled over to the shed and applied his eye to a hole in the timbers. McCoy's horse was tethered inside, pawing the ground impatiently, but there was no sign of its master. Disappointed, Farrell was about to creep back to where he assumed Parker was stationed when an idea occurred to him. The shed was open to the elements on the side furthest away from him, so he slipped round to examine the horse at close range. As he had anticipated, the saddle-pouches which he had last seen under McCoy's bunk at the ranch were draped over the animal's back. Surely, Farrell thought, these represented the one sure way of inducing McCoy to reveal himself. Without the money he was effectively lost whether he made it to Mexico or not. Farrell approached the horse, gave it a couple of reassuring pats to keep it quiet, and removed the pouches. Hefting them over his left shoulder, so as to keep his right arm free, he cautiously retraced his original route.

As Farrell got closer to the building where he believed McCoy was holed up he was able to make out the figure of Clem Parker kneeling against a fence through which he would presumably have a good view of any move McCoy tried to make. Exploiting whatever scanty cover he could find, Farrell circled closer until he was within hailing distance.

'I got the money, McCoy,' he shouted. 'You ain't getting away with anything so you might as well come out with your hands up.'

Farrell's voice echoed around the empty buildings, but there was no response from McCoy. After waiting for a few moments, he ducked his head down and scuttled across to join Parker at the fence.

'Son-of-a-bitch just isn't going to come out,' he muttered.

When Parker made no reply Farrell touched him on the shoulder.

'Clem?'

147

As Farrell's grip tightened in puzzlement at the other man's lack of response Parker's body fell backwards almost into his lap. Farrell yelped – less with surprise at the unexpected movement than at the sight of Parker's throat which had been slashed from ear to ear.

ELEVEN

Farrell recoiled in disgust from the disfigured corpse, but before he had time to gather his wits he heard a hoarse chuckle from close behind him. Turning his head he saw McCoy at the far end of the fence, six-shooter in hand.

'Neat job, eh, Farrell? The sucker never heard me coming.'

'Yeah. Just like the one you did on Sibley.'

'Pays to be handy with a knife when someone gets greedy. But right now, it's pistols that talk.'

McCoy motioned with his gun.

'On your feet, Farrell. I'm going to drill you full of lead.'

The situation seemed hopeless. Caught in a crouching position Farrell had no hope of drawing his Colt before McCoy could pull the trigger on him. In desperation he tried one last gambit. Instead of standing up he flattened himself to the ground, using Parker as a screen. McCoy's shot was almost instantaneous, but the bullet whacked vainly into Parker's already lifeless body. Before the smoke cleared and McCoy could fire again, Farrell had slicked Parker's gun out of its holster and unleashed a shot of his own. There was no time to aim and the shot went wide, slicing splinters from the timbers above McCoy's head. But it gave Farrell a split second to roll under the palings, get to his feet and sprint towards the safety of the adjacent building. Behind him he heard McCoy utter a furious oath.

He was within a few paces of shelter when McCoy fired again. The shot was aimed at his left shoulder and, at that close range, calculated to penetrate to his heart. But the pouch that he still had draped over his shoulder saved him. The bullet struck one of the heavy buckles and deflected into his upper arm. Unaware of his narrow escape from certain death Farrell was simply conscious of a jolt in his left arm and a sudden dull pain as if someone had landed him a violent punch on his biceps. Despite the deflection and partial protection of the leather pouch the impact of the bullet knocked him to his knees just as he was reaching the front of the building he had been making for.

He staggered upright, aware of the sound of McCoy's boots closing the distance between them, and ran along the creaking boards of the stoop. Giving no chance for McCoy to fire again into his retreating back he hurled himself through the doorway just as McCoy unleashed another shot that sent chips of dry timber scattering from the frame just inches from his head. But as Farrell reached the interior his luck finally ran out. The floorboards inside had entirely disintegrated and he found himself stepping into a void. With his footing totally lost, he sprawled helplessly in the dirt, rolling over on his back just in time to see the figure of his pursuer silhouetted outside the doorway.

Farrell still had Parker's pistol clasped in his hand. He raised it and fired desperately at the shadow looming outside. As the hammer clicked uselessly, Farrell felt a sickening lurch in the pit of his stomach. He had had no idea of how many shots Parker had already fired, and had now discovered – too late, of course – that the revolver's chamber was empty.

For a moment McCoy remained outside motionless, with pistol levelled.

'Nice try, Farrell. Pity you can't count.'

Disgusted with the catastrophic turn of events Farrell resigned himself to the worst.

'OK, McCoy, get it over with. Shoot, damn you.'

'Sure,' said McCoy. 'Anything to oblige. But I got to tell you it ain't going to be pleasant. I'm gonna shoot you in the gut, mister, and leave you to die slowly like the coyote bait you are.'

He lowered his aim towards Farrell's belt, but as his finger tightened on the trigger the rotten timbers beneath his boots collapsed under his weight in a shower of dust, sending him sprawling backwards with one foot inextricably caught between the floorboards. Farrell could risk no further mistake. He scrambled to his feet, drew his own pistol and fired down at the struggling figure in front of him. Uncertain in the half-light whether he had scored a hit he fired again, but this time the hammer clicked without result. His pistol, like Parker's, was now empty. McCoy had stopped struggling, but Farrell approached with caution only to find, with unutterable relief, that his last bullet had been decisive. A spreading patch of crimson on McCoy's shirt showed where he had been hit in the chest. Farrell prodded the body with the toe of his boot but there was no sign of life.

'Son-of-a . . .' he muttered, in disgust. Then, clutching his wounded arm, he stumbled off to find Finch.

The sheriff was lying where Farrell had left him.

'Hell of a lot of shooting back there,' he muttered as Farrell knelt down beside him. 'Are we back in business, or not?'

'Just about. McCoy's dead. But I'm afraid he got Clem.'

Finch shook his head in disappointment.

'Poor son-of-a-gun. I hope it was clean.'

'In a manner of speaking,' replied Farrell, seeing no point in troubling Finch with the unpleasant details of Parker's demise. A glance at the bloodstained boards under the sheriff's leg showed that he would be better off without any further shock. He decided to offer some good news instead.

'The money's safe,' he said, tapping the bulging saddle-pouches.

'So we haven't been wasting our time. You'll have a share of the reward money coming to you when we—'

'Hey,' protested Farrell, withdrawing his hand from the pouches as if they had contained rattlesnakes. 'I never did this for—'

'Take it easy, will you. I know you didn't. If you ain't the touchiest . . .'

There was an angry silence for a few moments.

'I see you took a shot yourself,' said Finch, pointing at Farrell's bloodstained shirtsleeve. 'The skunk really peppered us.'

'Nothing much,' lied Farrell, wishing that there were some way he could detach himself from the agonizing pain in his arm.

They spent the next half-hour bandaging each other up with the limited resources at their disposal. And only when this was completed did Farrell sit down and give further consideration to their situation. McCoy was dead and the money recovered, so their mission was accomplished. However. . . .

'Seems to me,' said Finch, suddenly voicing the gloomy thoughts that were already occupying Farrell's mind, 'that we're in something of a hole. We've got four horses, two dead bodies, we're both wounded, and we're miles from anywhere. You fancy spending the night here?'

'Nope.'

Farrell tried to keep any note of resignation out of his

voice. The fact was that although his own arm would just about make it without immediate attention, what he had seen of Finch's leg wound – not to mention the ugly scar across his head – made it obvious that the older man wouldn't survive long on horseback.

'Nope,' he repeated. 'But I think maybe you might have to. I can just about ride for help, but you shouldn't—'

'Hey,' protested Finch. 'Cut that out, mister. I'm not lying here with two corpses and all the rattlers in the territory for company while you—'

'OK. So let's hear your plan.'

'Well, I . . .'

A sudden spasm of pain from his leg stifled Finch's reply. They might have remained in a state of indefinite deadlock, had not the means of salvation appeared from the far horizon with a whirl of dust and the rumbling of wheels.

'Well, I'll be . . .' exclaimed Farrell jumping to his feet and waving his uninjured arm about frantically.

'I think we got ourselves a ride,' he called excitedly to Finch as the northbound stage rattled to an unscheduled stop beside them.

'What in tarnation's going on here?' demanded the driver as his suspicious companion levelled a shotgun at the two men. He peered down at them, apparently unable to believe the evidence of his own eyes.

'That you, Jade Finch?'

'Of course it is, you bonehead. And we need transport urgent. You got room for us on board?'

'Reckon so – always assuming you got the fare,' chuckled the driver. 'How far you going?'

'Look, cut out the wisecracks, will you. This is serious.'

The driver jumped down to examine them more closely.

'Jeez,' he muttered, when the state of their wounds

153

became apparent. 'We'll squeeze the sheriff inside if the other kind folks won't mind moving up a little.' He gestured to Farrell. 'And you on top.'

'Right,' said Farrell, satisfied with these arrangements which seemed better than anything that had been available a few minutes previously. 'Oh,' he added, almost as a casual afterthought. 'And we got two dead bodies as well . . .'

'That so?' replied the driver in a deadpan tone suggesting that nothing further would surprise him. 'You need a hearse, mister, not a stagecoach.'

The sudden opening of the bedroom door jolted Farrell out of a pleasant afternoon doze. He opened his eyes to find Beth Carney standing by the bedside.

'Sorry to disturb your siesta, Matt, but you got a visitor.'

'A visitor. . . ?'

'Of course, if you don't feel up to it . . . I mean, Doc Wilson said you were to take things real quiet.'

Farrell eased himself into a sitting position with difficulty and a visible wince. The arm from which Wilson had extracted a bullet in the early hours of the morning was decidedly painful and taped up in a way to discourage any significant movement.

'I'm all right,' he lied. 'Feel a bit of a fraud lying here, really.'

'Can't see why,' Beth retorted with asperity. 'Whole town's buzzing with what you and Jade got up to yesterday.'

'How is he?'

'He'll live, apparently. Might be a bit lame.'

'Oh. Guess I was lucky it was only my arm that got hit.'

'Yeah. But anyway you should take it quietly. Doc says you lost a lot of blood.'

'But this room. I mean, I can't . . .'

He gestured vaguely with his free arm. The room in the newly refurbished hotel had been supplied gratis by Beth as an aid to recovery and offered a degree of comfort – carpeted floor, chintz draperies, large feather bed – which he had rarely had the opportunity to savour before.

'For heaven's sake hush up. Stay as long as it takes. My late brother wasn't worth much, but I reckon I owe you something for nailing his killer.'

'You might regret that offer,' said Farrell with a smile. 'I could get used to this sort of pampering. Real nice place you got here. I'm surprised those Quakers never made a go of it.'

'Sharp enough on the accounting, but didn't have the first idea about how to make people comfortable. I guess that's Quakers for you. Should have stayed in Philadelphia.'

'Oh well, let's see my visitor.'

Beth withdrew and a minute or so later heavy footsteps approached along the passage outside. The door was opened without any preliminary knock.

'Why, Mr Ferguson.'

'Thought I'd come in and check up on you,' said Ferguson in a gruff voice. 'News reached the ranch this morning. Fine job you did.'

'Thanks.'

Ferguson stumped across the room and stood by the bedside with an air of slight embarrassment.

'Er, mind if I sit down?' he muttered after a brief pause.

'Help yourself,' said Farrell gesturing to a nearby chair.

When Ferguson had sat down he gave Farrell an appraising stare and then resumed the conversation.

'That arm hurting?'

'Some. Doc says it'll be OK. Bullet came out clean as a whistle. It's over there on the washstand if you want to . . .'

'No thanks. I just called in on Finch. If it's any consolation he's in an even worse state than you are.'

There was another silence as Ferguson fidgeted awkwardly with his hat. Then he spoke again.

'Look Farrell, I didn't just come to ask about your health.'

'Oh. Something else happened?'

'Not exactly. It's just that . . . Well, I've been rethinking the position at the ranch. The thing is, in just twenty-four hours I've lost two good men. Not that I'm making any excuses for Frank McCoy, mind,' he added hastily. 'But as a cattleman he was first rate. And then you quitting as well. Whole affair leaves me real short-handed.'

Farrell remained silent.

'So what I was coming to,' continued Ferguson, when it became clear that his ex-employee was not about to ease the conversation forward, 'was to ask whether you'd come back to the ranch.'

Farrell considered this proposal in silence for a moment. McCoy's death had removed his original reason for quitting, of course, but Pinedale Fork would still be full of all sorts of associations which it might be better to put behind him.

'I don't know,' he said at length. 'Seems to me you shouldn't have that much difficulty finding a hand to fill my bunk—'

'Fill your bunk?' interrupted Ferguson. 'I wasn't offering you your old job back.'

Farrell raised his eyebrows.

'Then what. . . ?'

'You're tarnation slow on the uptake at times, boy. Let's put it down to that injured arm. I was offering you McCoy's job, you dumb coyote. Ten bucks a week and your own room. Not as luxurious as you've got here of course. Now do you want it or not?'

'Oh,' said Farrell, biting his lip. 'I hadn't expected . . . I mean . . . that's real generous. But wait a minute. You got other experienced men out there who could easily take over. Wouldn't make much sense for me to come back muscling in on—'

'Oh Jesus, Farrell,' exploded Ferguson, 'you're real good at this modesty thing. Given any job on the ranch you can knock the others into a cocked hat. I know it, you know it.'

'Maybe, but all the same. . . .'

'Well,' said Ferguson rising from his seat. 'Let's have one final stab at putting it to you in terms you'll understand. Excluding your present . . . er . . . disability is there any man on the ranch you couldn't whip in a fair fight?'

Farrell pondered this unexpected question for a moment and then smiled.

'Guess not.'

'Fine,' said Ferguson decisively. 'That entitles you to the foreman's job. So do you want it, or not?'

'I reckon you just twisted my other arm,' chuckled Farrell. 'It's a deal.'

'Good. In that case I'll leave you to your next visitor.'

'My next. . . ?'

But Ferguson had already turned his back and left the room without any further comment. A minute or so later Farrell's face brightened considerably when the trim figure of Hetty Ferguson appeared in the doorway.

'Hello, Matt. All right to come in?'

'Sure,' said Farrell, hastily pulling up the lace counterpane to cover his bare torso.

'Pa just said you were coming back to the ranch,' said Hetty, settling herself uninvited on the bedside chair.

'Yeah. He kind of talked me into it. And anyway the foreman's job at ten bucks a week is too good to—'

'Only ten dollars a week? But didn't you haggle with him?' asked Hetty in tones of exasperation. 'Matt Farrell, you're a muttonhead. You must know you're worth more than that to Pa.'

'Well,' said Farrell with some discomfort. 'I didn't really think. I mean . . .'

'Well, let's put it down to that injured arm. It's only natural you'd be a bit confused with the chloroform and all.'

'What chloroform? Doc used his supply up on Finch.'

Farrell grimaced at this sudden recollection of the session he had spent on Doc Wilson's operating couch. Actually it was the only part of the night he could clearly remember after they had finally pulled out of High Stakes. The horses had been roped behind the stage, and the bodies of McCoy and Parker had somehow been lodged on the roof, after one of the paying passengers had vigorously objected to them being accommodated inside. Farrell himself spent the journey back to Pinedale Fork wedged on the front seat between the driver and his shotgun-toting companion. Even without the throbbing pain of his injured arm, the journey would have seemed interminable as the coach jolted and jarred its way along the trail. Give him a decent horse any time.

'. . . My goodness,' Hetty was saying, leaning forward. 'You mean he. . . . ?'

'Weren't nothing.'

He would have shrugged if his movements hadn't been so constricted by the bandaging. The truth was that he had passed out as soon as Wilson splashed surgical spirit on the wound, so he had been effectively absent for the subsequent ordeal of the forceps. But there was no need for Miss Hetty to know that, of course.

'Oh. Well, then you're doubly excused for not putting up a fight with Pa. Anyway, that can all be fixed when you're back at the ranch and we can have a serious talk about our – I mean – your future.'

158

'Hey,' protested Farrell, his eyes almost popping with sudden alertness. 'You shouldn't go talking like that, Miss Hetty. Mr Ferguson wouldn't take kindly to me—'

'Don't get agitated, Matt,' interrupted Hetty. 'It's bad for you in your condition.'

She leant forward and planted a light kiss on his forehead.

'You just leave Pa to me. I'm sure he'll come round to my way of thinking,' she said with a demure smile. 'After all, he usually does.'